Come to me Freely
BETH KERY

ELLORA'S CAVE
ROMANTICA PUBLISHING

An Ellora's Cave Publication

www.elloracave.com

Come To Me Freely

ISBN 9781419961045
ALL RIGHTS RESERVED.
Come To Me Freely Copyright © 2008 Beth Kery
Edited by Ann Leveille.
Photograph and cover art by Les Byerley.

Electronic book publication July 2008
Trade paperback publication 2012

With the exception of quotes used in reviews, this book may not be reproduced or used in whole or in part by any means existing without written permission from the publisher, Ellora's Cave Publishing, Inc.® 1056 Home Avenue, Akron OH 44310-3502.

Warning: The unauthorized reproduction or distribution of this copyrighted work is illegal. Criminal copyright infringement, including infringement without monetary gain, is investigated by the FBI and is punishable by up to 5 years in federal prison and a fine of $250,000. (http://www.fbi.gov/ipr/)

This book is a work of fiction and any resemblance to persons, living or dead, or places, events or locales is purely coincidental. The characters are productions of the author's imagination and used fictitiously.

The publisher and author(s) acknowledge the trademark status and trademark ownership of all trademarks, service marks and word marks mentioned in this book.

The publisher does not have any control over and does not assume any responsibility for author or third-party Web sites or their content.

COME TO ME FREELY
ଏ

Dedication

This is dedicated to J.S.P. and our memories of the "flats".

Chapter One

"I hope that I never see this much food in my house, again," Sarah McNeal said gruffly as she stood in front of her packed refrigerator.

Leigh inspected the dozens of casseroles, baked goods and desserts that covered Sarah's countertop. It was the first time she'd heard real grief in her mother-in-law's voice since her husband Jeff had died three days ago.

"I know. It was only a year ago that we were doing this same thing for Jim…and now Jeff," Leigh replied throatily.

"There was one other time that you and I laid food out like this, Leigh. Funny thing is that it was this same time of year — cold, hollow February."

"Oh God, Sarah. How could I have forgotten?"

Both women stood in silence for a moment, lost in their private memories of the time when Jim had the car accident that gave him a T-11 complete spinal cord injury, making him paraplegic and wheelchair dependent for life.

Jim and Leigh had been sixteen-year-old sweethearts at the time.

Sarah sighed. "I know you haven't, Leigh. Such a thing isn't easily forgotten." The small spasm of pain passing over Sarah's handsome features was her sole consolation to grief for the time being.

Leigh cleared her throat uncomfortably. She wanted to be strong for Sarah, not melt into a puddle around her. "After Jim died I tried to take things one day at a time. In the beginning I had to cut it down to just one hour at a time."

Sarah's sharp eyes flickered over to her daughter-in-law. Mourning just didn't suit her hardy personality. "Lord, I'm glad you're here."

Instead of trying to put the casserole dish she held in her hands into the crammed refrigerator, she set it down and started removing several others.

"You're right. Everything will come in its own time, whether I'm ready for it or not. All I can do is survive the moment. So I'm making an executive decision to send you over to Grandpa's with some of this food. It'll spoil if we leave it out until this afternoon and it'll freeze outside. You know how many people cared about Jeff. This house will be packed after the funeral and the least I can do is make sure people are fed properly."

Sarah was so preoccupied that it took her a moment to notice Leigh's unusual quietude. "Is that okay, Leigh? Maybe you wanted to rest for a while after driving in from Chicago. Oh, and you said that one of your patients had an emergency late last night..."

"Of course it's fine, Mom. I told you that I was coming down to help in any way I could."

"If you're sure... Now that I notice, you look a little pale," Sarah said with a furrowed brow.

But when Leigh insisted, Sarah finally nodded decisively. "Let's load up the pickup with some of this stuff then and you can drive that over. Don't want to take the chance of getting your beautiful car all messed up."

Five minutes later Sarah brought out the last casserole dish and laid it in the bed of the truck. "That should do it. It's a lot but Tre will have room. He probably doesn't keep anything in the refrigerator over there but pop and beer. He sponges a lot of his meals off of me when he's not eating that garbage they serve over at Casey's," Sarah said with a gruffness that didn't disguise the fondness in her voice. Leigh knew that her mother-in-law would throw a fit if her son didn't eat some of her home cooked meals.

"Tre knows who the best cook in the county is, that's all." Leigh smiled but it was only to hide her feeling of anxiety.

Tre.

It was the first time his name had passed her lips since Jim's funeral a year ago. And even then she hadn't been required to say his name much because she'd avoided him with a skill acquired from long years of practice.

Thinking about him was different. She'd thought about Tre more times than she cared to admit to herself.

The two-lane country road was well cleared of snow but still white and crunchy with early morning frost. Of course neither the farm nor the house that she headed toward was really "Grandpa's". Now that Jeff had died the entire four-thousand-eight-hundred acres of fertile farmland were Tre's. The McNeals had always referred to the twelve hundred acre stretch on the eastern border of the property that Tre owned as "Grandpa's" even though Leigh knew that Josh McNeal had been dead for years even before she met Jim when she was a girl. Tre had inherited that portion of the land when he was only twenty years old.

Leigh was always surprised anew as she studied the landscape near where she'd grown up in Shelby, Illinois. The land was so flat the eye could see for miles. The singular landscape of the "flats" was related to why it was considered to be one of the richest, most fertile farming areas on the planet. Glaciers had sat almost immobile on the land for tens of thousands of years, scraping the land as level as a tabletop but dumping enormous amounts of nutrients back into the soil at the same time.

Because of the featureless land and winter barrenness, she was able to see Tre's house for a full minute before she pulled into the long driveway. She studied the sprawling farmhouse and tried to still her racing heartbeat and turbulent thoughts.

She hadn't been alone with Tre for ten years.

And the last time they had been alone together was right here...in this very house.

When she saw the older model, dented sports car in Tre's driveway, some of her tension eased. Tre wasn't alone. She knew instinctively that it wasn't one of his vehicles. Tre was meticulous about the upkeep of his personal cars, just as he was about his horses, his home, his trucks and his farm equipment. When Leigh had first met him she'd assumed that his neatness was a result of his military training. But Sarah, Jeff and Jim had since told her that Tre had always been fastidious, even as a child. With his belongings and work habits anyway. When it came to his person Tre was insouciant.

Not that he needed to be concerned about his looks. Little imperfections like a long overdue haircut, a five o'clock shadow or dirty work boots and jeans only maximized his masculine appeal, never detracted from it.

As Leigh slid a casserole dish out of the bed of the truck she realized that Tre had made vast improvements on the old farmhouse since the last time she'd seen it. The dark green shutters on every window were freshly painted, as was the white wood siding. He'd even restored and painted the huge porch swing on the wraparound veranda. Leigh acknowledged for the first time that it was a beautiful old home, a genuine slice of Americana.

Even though she stood at the forest green front door for a full twenty seconds when she did finally knock it was with a firm briskness. After almost two minutes and several attempts she finally heard an inside deadbolt sliding open.

She took an unsteady breath and braced herself to see Tre.

Instead she found herself facing a half-naked young woman. Leigh blinked. Her brain scrambled to interpret the image of this attractively mussed stranger who appeared to be dressed only in one of Tre's shirts. It fell on her somewhere in the middle of bare, firm thighs. Her breasts swelled generously above the mere three buttons that had been fastened.

"Oh...good morning," Leigh finally managed when she realized that the woman was eyeing her with sleepy, suspicious brown eyes.

"Yeah, I guess so. What time is it anyway?"

"It's about seven. Is Tre around?"

"Sure. He's in bed." The look that the woman gave Leigh let her know that Tre was where most sane people were at this hour of the morning.

"Oh, I'm sorry. He's usually an early riser. His mother and I just assumed—"

"Most nights he probably doesn't put away close to a full bottle of bourbon," the woman interrupted with a harsh bark of laughter.

"Who is it?"

Leigh stilled at the sound of the deep, sleep-roughened voice. The woman who had answered the door glanced over to the right and shrugged.

"Hell if I know, Tre."

Leigh noticed that her voice had gone from bordering on rudeness to a sultry drawl in a split second. Her spine straightened indignantly.

"Sarah asked me bring some things over, Tre," Leigh stated with a matter-of-factness she was far from feeling. She didn't hear him approach but abruptly the dark green door swung back.

She held up her chin as she stared into Tre McNeal's piercing blue eyes.

"What are *you* doing here?"

"Well good morning to you too. Didn't your mother tell you I was coming for the funeral?"

"Yeah. I never expected that you'd be coming over here though."

Leigh swallowed. His face had been cold and expressionless when he said it. Still Leigh knew. He was referring to the last time she'd been to the farmhouse. He was subtly telling her that he knew how she'd been carefully avoiding him since then.

"Sarah asked me to bring over food to put in your refrigerator. Hers is packed and she needs the food for after the funeral," she explained evenly. For a few seconds Tre just stared at her, unmoving. "Tre, can I please come in? It's freezing out here."

He moved back slightly, signaling permission if not a welcome. Leigh rushed past him. The sooner she got this over with the better. She noticed that Tre's formerly sleepy bedmate looked alert now and completely irritated by Leigh's intrusion. Leigh met her stare, daring her to say something, especially when Leigh was on such a righteous mission.

She didn't need to look up to know that Tre had followed her into the kitchen. Leigh didn't want to admit that she was afraid to look at him. His sole concession to clothing consisted of a pair of faded, partially fastened jeans. Leigh knew for a fact that he'd just pulled them on before he came to the door and that he wasn't wearing a damn thing beneath them but warm, smooth male skin.

It was bad enough that she avoided his person. She couldn't refuse to look at him indefinitely as well. Her voice sounded brisk and matter-of-fact when she spoke.

"Are you going to help me or not?"

Leigh's heart drummed uncomfortably in her ears in the ensuing silence. Her eyes were drawn to him against her will.

She went completely still. Maybe she *should* consider not looking at him indefinitely. Especially now…in his present state of undress.

Leigh had never understood how God had seen fit to gift Tre with such a disproportionate amount of pure male sexuality. Technically Jim had been the more classically handsome of the two brothers. Her husband's features had been more regular, more harmonious in their arrangement. Tre's face was harder than Jim's. And the last word that came to Leigh's mind when she sought to define Tre's expression as he studied her from beneath raven black brows was "harmonious".

"Is there a lot more?"

"Yes, the bed is full of food that people have been bringing over."

Despite her request, the only movement Tre made as he leaned indifferently against the countertop was the stirring of his thumb. The idle gesture brought Leigh's eyes downward. His arms were crossed loosely over his chest and his right hand circled a steely, work-hewn biceps. The thumb fluttered less than an inch away from an erect dark brown nipple.

"Just forget it," she muttered as fury unexpectedly bubbled to the surface. "I can see that you're otherwise occupied." Her eyes sliced over to the woman who had just entered the kitchen. She stormed past him toward the front door.

Tre's arm snaked out and grabbed her wrist with lightening speed. He jerked her body against him.

"I know the horse is damn high but do you think you could manage to get off it without breaking your pretty ass, Leigh?"

For a long second their gazes held. He'd breathed out the question so ominously but so quietly, and their faces were poised so close together that Leigh doubted the other woman had heard. Leigh felt her lower lip fall away from the upper one in a motion that felt suspiciously like anticipation as she stared up into his fiery eyes.

"Tre, are we going back to bed or not?"

Leigh yanked at her wrist, feeling as if she'd been temporarily granted freedom from the snare that was Tre McNeal when his attention fractured at his lover's peevish question. She had almost made it to the hallway entrance when Tre uttered her name in a whip-like tone of voice she wasn't likely to ignore even in her present emotional state.

Her feet paused but she didn't turn around.

"Just let me talk to Julie for a second and throw on some clothes. I'll be out to help you in a minute."

Leigh convinced herself that she couldn't care less where the couple was the next time she came barreling through Tre's front door. But that didn't stop her from noticing that they were nowhere to be seen. Nor did it prevent her from softening her footsteps on the way out the door again to see if she could locate them in the house with her sensitized ears. When she heard Tre's deep voice and an answering feminine reply emanating from down the hallway that led to what Leigh knew from experience to be the master bedroom, she flung the front door open and left it wide this time.

Tre had the money to pay for a little wasted heat.

Leigh passed him on the front steps a few minutes later. He'd dressed in a white T-shirt, an open flannel shirt and dark brown work boots. He wasn't wearing a coat but he seemed impervious to the February chill. She passed Julie next, clumping down the front stairs in a pair of high-heeled boots. Her brown curly hair spilled over the collar of a short black leather jacket that was hardly suited to the twelve-degree temperature.

"Hey, I'm sorry about the welcome earlier. Tre and I were out late last night. He told me you were his sister-in-law."

Leigh paused on the stairs. Julie's pale face still looked petulant but at least she'd made the point of trying. Which was more than Leigh had attempted. Leigh sighed and put out her hand in greeting.

"I'm sorry for getting you out of bed so early. I'm Leigh McNeal." She bristled when she saw the way that Julie suspiciously inspected her outstretched hand. Then she recalled that the custom of women shaking hands in greeting was relatively uncommon in the farm country of central Illinois. Julie eventually took her hand limply.

"Julie Garretson."

"Are you related to the Gibsonville Garretsons?"

"Yeah," Julie said noncommittally. Her brown eyes traveled over Leigh's face, hair and dark blue, belted, cashmere coat. "I wouldn't have guessed you would know about the Garretsons. You grow up around here?"

Leigh nodded. She sensed Tre's approach, confirming it when she saw that she became a complete nonentity in Julie's attention field. When she came outside the front door a few seconds later she pointedly averted her eyes from the sight of Julie straining up on her tiptoes to kiss Tre in parting.

Neither Tre nor Leigh spoke for the next few minutes as they emptied the truck. When Tre entered the kitchen with the two last dishes Leigh was bent in front of his refrigerator trying to fit in everything. He didn't only have pop and beer chilling like Sarah had predicted. Quite a few other food items and condiments lined the shelves. Fortunately Tre's appliances weren't the ancient, olive green ones that Leigh recalled being here ten years ago. His refrigerator was a sleek, gigantic, stainless steel number that she and most of her upscale neighbors in the Gold Coast neighborhood of Chicago would have loved to possess. She didn't meet his eyes when he handed her the last casserole dish.

"So we're reversing the whole process after the funeral?" Tre asked when Leigh stood.

Her eyes skittered to his reluctantly when she heard the *we're*. She hadn't thought beyond surviving this difficult encounter.

"That's the idea." Her eyes skated away from his almost immediately. She glanced around the warm, modernized kitchen.

"Grandpa's place looks fantastic, Tre. I can't believe all the changes you've made."

"Never planned on being here again to notice, did you?"

Her arms crowded around herself when her body convulsed with a sudden tremor. Leigh told herself that she would never grow used to the bitter winter on the exposed flatlands of the Midwest. For a moment, neither of them moved nor spoke. Finally Leigh met Tre's eyes.

"I'm sorry about Jeff."

A muscle twitched slightly in his lean jaw but otherwise he was expressionless.

"You loved him too," he finally said.

Leigh nodded. It was still hard to meet his eyes but it wasn't unbearable. "He wasn't my blood father though. It isn't the same."

Tre shifted restlessly against the kitchen counter. "I was sorry to hear about Charlie. I would have attended his service but…"

Leigh nodded. "I know. You were still out in D.C. then, just starting up your business." She referred to the security software business that he had run successfully for years before Jeff had begun ailing and required Tre's help managing the huge farm. Leigh understood from Sarah that he'd sold his business at an enormous profit and still owned quite a few shares in it.

"It wasn't because the business was more important. By the time Mom told me about your dad, Charlie had already been buried."

Leigh sighed. "It's okay. It was a small service. My mother purposefully made a point of not inviting the Casey's faction. She undoubtedly considered you to be an honorary member of that group," Leigh said wryly, referring to the local bar that her father used to frequent far too often."

"Doris is such a bitch. Some of those guys at Casey's were his lifelong friends."

Leigh didn't even bother to defend her mother. Doris Peyton was a hard, bitter woman. She also didn't remind Tre that Charlie's best friend at Casey's had been the ever-full bottle of vodka.

Tre already knew that too.

"It was better to have a private service. Charlie would never have had the turnout of someone like Dad, someone who was so respected in the community."

When the impact of her own words sank in Leigh turned away and began straightening up the few items that she'd left on Tre's counter when she'd consolidated for storage. She felt vulnerable when she realized how she called her own father by his first name while automatically referring to Jeff McNeal as *Dad*.

Her breath caught when she felt Tre's hand on her upper arm, stilling her restless straightening. "I know how you felt about Dad. Why do you always have to deny your feelings?"

Leigh looked up in dazed disbelief at the unexpected accusation. He was standing close. Too close. She imagined that she felt the heat coming off his body. She didn't need to imagine that she could breathe in his scent. Despite his unshowered state and late night of drinking and sex he smelled wonderful—raw and male. The realization made her eyes widen.

"I never saw you cry a tear at Jim's funeral," Tre said.

"Are you implying that I didn't grieve for Jim?"

He smirked. "I'd never dare to insinuate something like that about your precious Jim…or about Dad for that matter. I'm just asking why you run from strong feelings. You always have to be in control, don't you?"

"Tre, let go," she murmured calmly enough but she couldn't disguise the tremor that laced through her voice.

"No. Still playing it safe, huh, Leigh? Taking the path of least resistance? Answer me," Tre insisted with a laser-like intensity that Leigh had only heard from him a few times in her life. Her eyes squeezed shut but the memory pushed itself into her awareness anyway.

You're mine, Leigh.

"I loved both Jim and your father deeply. Why would I deny it?" Her face pulled tight with unexpressed emotion when she suddenly found herself wrapped in his arms.

"What are you doing?" she asked desperately against his flannel shirt.

"What do you think? I'm consoling you. You wouldn't let me come near you when Jim died. I wasn't there when Charlie died. Now Dad is gone too. What's wrong with us finding some comfort in each other's arms? We've both lost people we love," Tre said hoarsely into her hair.

The intense emotion that rose in Leigh's chest frightened her like nothing she'd ever experienced before. She choked and gasped when the feeling gripped at her throat. She recognized the emotion as grief but it wasn't for the loss of Jim or Jeff or Charlie. Her head shook in denial of it but a sob escaped her lips anyway. Tre continued to hold her fast, forcing her to feel it, blocking her from everything *but* feeling it. Leigh struggled against him but his arms were like bands of steel.

"Damn it, Tre, let me *go!*"

"Shut up, Leigh," he muttered starkly. Leigh saw the telling flash of fire in his eyes but the realization came too late for her to move.

His mouth covered hers urgently.

Her cry was like that of an animal's when it feels the death strike of a predator. Only Tre's kiss didn't kill, it stirred her to life with alarming accuracy.

His mouth slanted over hers and refamiliarized itself with every texture, taste and contour. He didn't seem to care one way or another if she responded to him willingly but his white-hot intensity demanded a reciprocal reaction from Leigh, and she gave it. When she felt his insistent fingers urge her jaw downward she yielded to him without conscious thought. The primitive parts of her brain instinctively recognized the scent and taste of Tre even while her rational mind was blind and fumbling.

Tre bent over her and sent his tongue deep. Just before Leigh had knocked on his door this morning he'd been lying in bed staring up at the ceiling, hung over and irritated as hell with himself while Julie had knelt next to him, her head bobbing over his lap, trying her damndest to coax a better mood out of him. It had been working but more out of sheer perseverance and enthusiasm on Julie's part than any real interest on Tre's.

But all it took was one look at Leigh—never mind one deep inhalation of her singular scent or one taste of her—and his body awakened to a fevered sexual pitch, fully primed and ready to mate after only seconds of looking into her startled, depthless green eyes.

Fuck. Why did it have to be her that drove him so wild? Why Leigh...always Leigh?

He swallowed the sexy sound that she made deep in her throat. When she slid her tongue sinuously against his he gave a low groan of masculine appreciation.

Once he knew that he had her where he wanted her, he proceeded to slay her with gentleness. He sipped at her lips, molding their flesh together, savoring her taste. He kissed her with more restraint but his hunger swelled monumentally. His cheeks flexed, making her tongue his captive within his mouth where he could stroke it and caress it with his lips, tongue and teeth at his leisure.

She moaned shakily at the sexual torment.

Even through the bulk of her winter coat Leigh could feel the hard planes of his body. She'd gravitated toward his masculine vibrancy from the first moment she'd met Tre. She pressed closer to the heat that always seemed to resonate from his fiery core. Her movement into him must have struck Tre as unsatisfactory. He reached down and roughly whipped open the belt that closed her coat. His hands slipped behind her lower back and brought her against him hard.

They shared a groan of arousal when their bodies sealed together, separated only by the relatively thin layers of their clothing. He raised his hands to her breasts and palmed her surely, the caress ending with his thumbs curling around her distended nipples. A low growl vibrated his throat at the sensation. He pinched both the hard tips lightly at the same time that he thrust his hips, pushing his cock into the soft harbor between her thighs.

Leigh moaned in sharp desire and rising misery. She pushed herself out of his arms and staggered back.

For several seconds they stared at each other over the distance of three or four feet. Tre got control of his ragged breathing sooner than Leigh did but his eyes still looked stormy. His voice was paradoxically cold.

"What's wrong?"

A small cry of disbelief leaked past her lips. Her sluggish mind fought for a viable answer. What had she been thinking to let him kiss her that way? He'd just been naked in bed with another woman less than twenty minutes ago. The thought made her teeth clench with rage.

"I can still smell her on you."

He shrugged after a prolonged pause.

"I'll go shower."

"How-how dare you?" Leigh practically choked on the words.

His nostrils flared with rising anger. "I'd dare much more for the chance to purge you from my blood once and for all."

Leigh blinked. Had he really just said that? Had he really planned to take her to bed under these circumstances? On the day of his father's funeral?

"What about that woman? Julie?"

"I just picked her up at Casey's last night, Leigh. It's not like she's the one true love of my life," he muttered with a hard tilt to his lips and a soft bark of laughter.

Leigh shook her head slowly. Her mouth opened and shut but she wasn't capable of producing words. Rage caused her brain to short-circuit.

Tre laughed mirthlessly. "What? Busy coming up with a morality sermon, Leigh? Going to lecture me on the sins of the flesh? Spare me, princess. Just because you play the part of saint to perfection doesn't give you the right to judge me. It just confirms that you're a great actress. You and I both know things are flowing hot between your legs right now. Why deny it?"

"You are such a...caveman...artifact...*pig!*" Leigh sputtered. How could she have let him get to her in this way? "Just stay away from me, Trevor McNeal! I'm not one of your playthings."

"As if you'd ever bend that stiff backbone of yours enough to make a decent one."

Leigh flinched.

Tre's eyes flashed but his expression remained stony.

Her hands shook when she found the ties to her coat and knotted them firmly around her. She never glanced back at him as she headed for Tre's front door.

* * * * *

They sat on either side of Sarah later that afternoon at the funeral.

Tre ached at the loss of his father. He'd admired him more than Jeff McNeal had ever known. Despite the outrageous things that he'd said to paint himself black to Leigh this morning, Tre had long tried to emulate his father's strong work ethic, his common sense ideals about right and wrong and his innate decency to his fellow human beings. Tre may have had to struggle with his wild, rebellious spirit on many an occasion but Jeff McNeal had always stood as a constant touchstone of stability and wisdom.

Maybe that was why he'd behaved so abysmally with Leigh this morning. He'd lost all guideposts of decency.

He glanced over at her. Unconsciously, his jaw clenched again. No. No matter how much he'd like to make an excuse for himself, even if his father were still alive Tre likely would have still lost all vestige of control once he was alone with Leigh.

He hated himself for it. He hated Leigh for it too.

That was the problem. Ever since he'd first laid eyes on her when she was only eighteen years old, Tre had lost his ability to direct his own mind with any degree of rationality. Just looking at Leigh sitting there so coolly, the way she held herself with so much regal containment, made him sweat. He honestly couldn't have said if his visceral response came from fury or pure, unmitigated lust.

He only knew that he had a deep, ugly urge to break her.

Tre figured it was no wonder he became a cyclone of whirling, discordant emotion whenever she was present. He'd like to think that his misbehavior last night—drinking exorbitantly past his normal limit and bedding a complete stranger—was because of the emotional upheaval of Jeff's death. But Tre knew better. He'd been spoiling for a fight, mind-numbing intoxication and the brief, merciful forgetfulness of a blistering orgasm ever since Sarah had told him that Leigh was coming to the funeral.

Leigh Peyton would undoubtedly be the death of him.

Tre refused to call her by his own family name, by his brother Jim's name. To him she would always be Leigh Peyton. Images of her leaning over Kingmaker's stall and brushing her fingers across his horse's nose rose briefly to haunt him. For a second he saw her as clearly as he had on that warm summer day ten years ago, envisioned the dazed expression in her wide eyes as she looked up at him.

Kingmaker isn't mean or cruel. You're wrong about him.

Tre's eyes automatically shifted to Leigh to covertly see how the woman compared to the girl of his imagination. Both images were stunning in their impact but Tre had to admit that Leigh had accomplished what he would have sworn once was an utter impossibility.

She'd become even more beautiful than his well-guarded memories of her. Tre swallowed bitterly and determinedly glanced away.

The elegant woman who sat not five feet away from him was not the kind of common, short-lived beauty that one typically found in the fertile farmlands of central Illinois. She may have grown up here but Tre had known from the start Leigh wasn't *of* here. He wondered at the mysteries of genetics whenever he looked at Leigh and saw the proud lines of her back, shoulders and cheekbones, the glossy dark brown hair that contrasted so strikingly with pale, flawless skin, the graceful, soft hands, the ripe, thrusting breasts, the slender, coltish quality of her long legs, the sexy swell of her round hips and ass…

Tre stopped himself irritably. How had a woman like Leigh ended up being born to Charlie and Doris Peyton in a sleepy, backwater Midwest farm town?

That this woman who was obviously formed for passion had chosen to sacrifice her life to martyrdom only infuriated Tre further. He cursed himself mentally when he realized that he'd just implied it would have taken a saint to marry his brother just because he'd been paraplegic. But of course Leigh had to carry her point a thousand steps further, devoting her life as a physiatrist at a spinal cord injury rehabilitation unit to saving every individual whom she treated. She did it not by curing spinal cords that had been irrevocably severed but by reforming the habits and attitudes of the injured and their families, never satisfied until the person in the wheelchair accepted him or herself as a fully viable, equal person in society.

Tre knew how it must have killed Leigh that Jim died of complications associated with sepsis. Jim had been doing skin care and pressure relief to prevent the sores that could progress to poisonous, mortal infections since his own rehabilitation stay when he was only sixteen years old. The fact that Jim had acquired a bone deep sore at age twenty-seven said nothing about Leigh's skills as a doctor and everything about Jim's growing depression. Leigh was no more responsible for Jim's skin care and pressure relief than she was for brushing his teeth every day. Jim had been fiercely independent since he'd come home from rehab twelve years ago.

But despite Jim's years of steadfast strength and Leigh's intelligence and dedication as a doctor, they hadn't been able to save Jim in the end. Tre became aware of a leaden sensation in his chest as he listened to Pastor Morrison read a passage from the Bible.

The reason he was so infuriated with Leigh was that she hadn't devoted herself to *him*. Wasn't that the ugly truth of it?

His face hardened. Yeah. That was pretty much the butt ugly truth.

His eyes flashed over to her proud profile with restrained fury. God he'd love to bend that stiff spine of hers, preferably in order to accommodate his cock while he fucked her in any number of positions, a few of which might even be possible in some place other than his imagination. He figured he was the world's foremost expert on fantasy-fucking Leigh Payton.

But why did it have to be a fantasy? he wondered abruptly. What did he have to lose by seducing Leigh? Not a damn thing. There was nothing between them at this point in their lives but the bitter taste of regret and a residual lust that likely wouldn't have the strength to outlast two good rounds.

Well, maybe three… Three hard, sweaty…*purging* fucks.

Perhaps that would get Leigh Payton out of his blood and recapture his lost sanity once and for all.

Chapter Two
ಸಾ

The chill between them when they returned to Tre's house to retrieve the food was so palpable that Leigh considered leaving her coat on. She cleared her throat uncomfortably after she followed Tre into his kitchen.

Why did a room's dimensions always seem to shrink when Tre was in it?

"I thought it might be helpful to Sarah if we heated up a few of the casseroles here to save her oven space. They'll stay warm in our cars," she informed the countertop to the right of where Tre stood. Her eyes flickered over to him when he didn't speak for several seconds. Leigh wasn't sure if she was glad or disappointed when he merely nodded once and turned on his oven.

"I'm going out to the stable," he said gruffly after he'd helped Leigh pull a few dishes out of the refrigerator.

Several minutes with his horses seemed to sooth his stormy spirit.

On the way back to the house he glanced up and caught Leigh watching him from the window over the kitchen sink. He paused then resumed more slowly. Much to his surprise she didn't break their mutual stare.

Leigh was painfully aware of the noises that Tre made as he entered the side door to the farmhouse. She gave a small smile when she heard a heavy stomp followed by the sound of him tapping his feet briskly against the stair.

He'd looked sinfully handsome and completely comfortable wearing the dark gray suit that he'd donned for his father's funeral. Leigh had to remind herself that he'd probably dressed like that regularly when he ran his own business after leaving the Navy. But she also knew that Tre would prefer to be wearing his work boots and jeans right now, just as she knew that he didn't like having to spend so much effort getting snow off of his footwear. If he had it his way his work boots would likely be tracking snow on the kitchen floor at this moment.

When Tre entered the kitchen Leigh hadn't moved away from her position by the sink but she was facing him. She'd tucked one of his dishtowels into the belt around her waist in order to protect the understated, expensive-looking black cashmere wrap dress that she wore. Her arms were crossed beneath her breasts defensively. Tre didn't remove his eyes from her wary face.

"Are we about ready to go?"

Leigh nodded. "I'll take out the casseroles in a minute."

His eyebrows rose mockingly. "Is there something you want to say?"

At first he thought he'd successfully cowed her. But if he'd thought that for a split second then he'd definitely forgotten the essence of Leigh—inches and inches of sensual, soft silk draped over hard steel. When she finally spoke he heard the tremor in her voice even before he processed the content of her question.

"Is-is Kingmaker out there?"

He paused at the unexpected question.

"Kingmaker's gone, Leigh. I never got a chance to tell you. We barely spoke at Jim's funeral—"

"Gone? You mean he's *dead*?"

Her green eyes widened with shock when he nodded once.

"He acquired a respiratory virus two years ago. It became so severe that it affected him neurologically," Tre explained.

"But..." Leigh paused when she felt a splash of wetness on her cheeks. She swiped at the tears distractedly.

"Kingmaker was only twelve years old! He was so strong and fierce and full of life. How could he be *gone*?"

When a spasm of pain convulsed her narrow rib cage Tre found he'd crossed the kitchen without ever consciously telling himself to move.

Her wounded cry fell across his lapel. She shuddered with grief, the depth of her emotion leaving her frightened and raw. Her attempts at logic and control tried valiantly to surmount her misery but her feelings were too strong. Rational thought splintered and was tossed like flotsam on waves of intense emotion.

"You and…you and Kingmaker…you…"

"Shhh," Tre murmured. He grimaced slightly when he heard the way the words ripped at her throat so violently. He held her to him tightly while she cried.

By slow degrees Leigh became aware of the cocoon of warmth that Tre created around her. At some point during her tumult her arms had encircled his waist. She gave a small murmur of concern when she realized how wet she'd made his crisp white dress shirt.

Tre noticed her wayward focus.

"Leave it," he ordered gruffly.

Leigh felt his hand press her head back to where it had been resting on his chest. She rubbed her cheek idly against him as her sobs slowly began to quiet.

Tre gave himself permission not to think. For a minute or so his world narrowed to the sensation of holding Leigh—the way her body trembled, her hauntingly familiar scent, how pale the scalp of her part was next to her dark brown hair. When he knew that her storm had passed, and when he felt a subtle tension begin to rise in her, he forced himself to back away from her warm, supple body.

His arms refused to let go though, leaving her in their protective circle.

"Okay?" His breath was warm against her upturned face.

For the first time in minutes Leigh met his gaze. His face was hard and expressionless but his striking blue eyes were alight with emotion.

"I'm all right."

She shifted away from him uncomfortably.

"I don't know why I got upset about it. Why did I get so upset about it?" she wondered with rising confusion.

"Maybe because you were holding back the sadness for a hell of lot more than a horse's death. Kingmaker was just the final straw."

For a few seconds their gazes met and held. Emotion rose in her throat all over again. She looked away with effort.

"You're right. It's been a hard day. We should go. Your mother will wonder about us," she murmured.

* * * * *

As the sun began to set over the McNeal farm that evening there were only five guests' cars left in the driveway. Hours ago, cars had lined either side of the rural route that led to Sarah and Jeff's home for a half a mile in each direction. Sarah had expressed her gratitude for the outpouring of heartfelt sympathies hundreds of times that evening, and Leigh knew that her mother-in-law's feelings were completely genuine each and every time.

Leigh kept as busy as possible making sure that food and drink were plentiful while Sarah and Tre greeted guests and accepted their respects.

She watched Tre covertly as she refilled a bowl with some crackers. He laughed as a farmer told him a story about when he and Jeff were fourteen-year-old hellions. Throughout the afternoon Leigh had come to realize that Jeff's eldest son had acquired his father's gift for recalling people's names, faces and stories and making them feel listened to and special during conversations.

There were so many things she didn't know about Tre. The small peek at an undiscovered aspect of his complex character admittedly fascinated her.

The laughter still mingled on Tre's lips when his eyes abruptly met hers. She tensed, expecting him to go cold. But his gaze remained warm. His disarming smile even widened slightly. Her hand froze over the bowl of crackers. Their first peaceful exchange in years was interrupted by Adam Taylor, a rangy, good-looking local who had been in the same year of school as Leigh and Jim.

Tre's expression did stiffen then.

"You sure do look prettier and prettier every time that I see you, Leigh," Adam complimented as he grabbed a cracker and munched on it. "It must be kind of hard for those crazy people to have such an attractive doctor, huh?"

Leigh didn't know whether to be offended or to laugh. Considering what she knew about Adam's relative harmlessness however, she eventually opted for the latter.

"I'm a *physiatrist*, Adam, not a psychiatrist."

"Oh, right," Adam said with a dazed look that clearly communicated that he was still completely in the dark as to what she did for a living.

Across the room, Sarah approached her son after the older farmer had said his goodbyes. "Well, that's almost everyone, I guess. Except for Adam Taylor over there. I guess Jeff would be surprised to know that Adam was one of his most steadfast mourners," Sarah said with amused weariness. It had been one of the longest, most difficult days of her life.

"One of Leigh's most steadfast admirers, more like," Tre muttered. His lips pressed together in irritation even though he knew instinctively that Leigh wasn't interested in the likes of Adam Taylor. He still didn't like to see her laugh in such a carefree way with another man when he knew he didn't have the power to make her look that way.

Sarah's amused expression faded to thoughtfulness. "How do you think Leigh looks, Tre?"

Tre shrugged. "What do you mean? She looks like she always does."

"She's thinner than she was at Jim's funeral. And she's pale too. Poor girl was in the emergency room last night with one of her patients before she drove all the way here."

Tre tried to study Leigh with a measure of objectivity as she bantered with Adam and sipped a glass of iced tea. Now that his mother mentioned it he saw the pallor of her cheeks, the light shadows beneath her eyes, a waist so thin that he probably could span it with his hands.

"Maybe she's just tired. She's staying on the farm for a while, isn't she?"

"She said she was leaving Sunday morning."

"You should try to talk her into staying longer, Mom. Let her get rested up," Tre said brusquely.

If Leigh stayed, great. If that kiss this morning was any indication they had some unfinished business together. If she didn't stay though—no sweat off his back. Tre figured he'd grown calloused to her elusive appearances in his life and the disappearances that inevitably followed.

Sarah sighed. "I'll try to talk her into it. You know how stubborn she can be."

Tre gave a mirthless bark of laughter at the stark understatement. He noticed his mother's sharp, speculative look.

"Let me help you and Leigh clean up, Mom. I'm supposed to be meeting someone later tonight."

* * * * *

Leigh felt far from stubborn or feisty that evening after everyone had left and she helped Tre and Sarah straighten up the kitchen. She felt beaten and weary and…heartsore. When she stood after storing the last of the dishes in a lower cabinet, Sarah reached out to her.

"You go on to bed, now, Leigh. You look completely done in."

A protest stilled on Leigh's lips when she noticed the steely look in Tre's eyes. He was expecting her to be contradictory. Leigh resolutely removed one of Sarah's half-aprons that she'd borrowed to cover her dress.

Tre didn't know her as well as he thought he did. Her eyes stung and her throat was beginning to feel sore. It had been a long, trying day and she'd been awake since two o'clock in the morning. "I think I will. I might be coming down with a cold or something."

"Well you just sleep in tomorrow for as long as you like, now. You go on too, Tre. I'll be fine and I know you have a date."

Leigh would have paid good money to make it so that her gaze didn't flicker up to meet Tre's at that moment. His eyes were like glowing embers as he watched her from across the kitchen.

Who was he seeing tonight? Julie? The thought of him spending another night in bed with that pretty little minx made her stomach churn.

"Good night, Sarah," Leigh whispered as she gave her mother-in-law a tender kiss and a hug. "Don't hesitate to wake me if you need me.

"Good night, Tre," she said shortly, refusing to make eye contact with him before she left the room.

"Leigh."

She paused halfway down the darkened hallway a few seconds later when she heard Tre call her name.

For a moment she just looked at the floor without turning around. When she finally did she was taken aback by how close he was standing. He seemed impossibly tall in the low-ceiling hallway. His face looked shadowed in the dim light.

"I don't want to fight with you, you know," he murmured.

Leigh bit her lower lip anxiously. The remnants of his spicy cologne mixed with his rich, masculine scent filtered subtly into her nostrils, making her slightly dizzy.

"You could have fooled me, Tre."

"You were the one who came prancing over to my house this morning with that gigantic chip on your shoulder," he accused in a muted voice.

Her cheeks flushed with renewed anger. "*You* were the one who tried to humiliate me by pawing me and then suggesting that I get into a bed that was still warm from another woman's body. If you don't want to fight with me then I can't imagine what the hell else you were doing!" she hissed furiously.

He shook his head in rising disgust. "I would think it was obvious what the hell I was doing. The same damn thing I've been trying to do since I first laid eyes on your ass ten years ago."

His hoarse whisper reverberated in the still hallway along with the sound of her blood pounding in her ears.

"*Nice*, Tre," she eventually murmured sarcastically. "Jeff would be *so* proud if he heard you talking this way."

"Uh uh, princess," he muttered tensely at the same time that he halted her attempt to walk away. His hand splayed over her lower back, pushing her body tightly into his. He waited until her wary gaze met his. "Self-righteous indignation would only work if I had any honor left. God knows you took that away from me years ago."

A hurt cry slid past her lips before he bent to stifle it with his mouth. He kissed her brutally, heedless of her struggles to free herself from his arms.

Tre would have been the first to admit that he was utterly and completely selfish at that moment. But the sure knowledge couldn't save him.

His hands spanned her narrow waist and sank down over her curving hips. His fingers flexed greedily into her ass. His cock surged into painful, taut readiness at the sensation of her round, firm flesh in his palms. He flexed his hips, pressing himself into her soft mound and belly.

God, she was just as lush and sweet as she had been ten years ago.

More so.

Lust stabbed into his flesh like a cruel, flaming blade.

Leigh couldn't have said at what point her muffled cries of fury became low moans of desperate desire but the alteration wasn't gradual nor was it partial. Tre had never inspired mediocrity in her. For Leigh, Tre meant all or nothing. She had learned early on that her only choices were to shut herself away from him completely or risk becoming enslaved.

Her fingers traced his broad shoulder and found their way beneath the collar of his shirt, eager for the sensation of vibrant, smooth skin. When he thrust his erection into her giving flesh she pressed back, grinding her sex against him with small undulations of her hips. He groaned into her mouth at the same time that he pushed her into the wall. Leigh welcomed his weight as he pressed into her from thigh to breast, glorying at how his hard, masculine angles felt against her feminine curves, the perfection of their fit striking her poignantly.

The anguished sound she made in her throat had its origins deep in her soul.

Her low cry reverberated through Tre, garnering his attention when little else could have penetrated his thick lust. He tore his mouth from hers, leaning back a scant inch so that he could examine her expression.

He could have taken her then. The evidence was clear in her shiny, lust-glazed eyes.

But the light turned on over the stairs filtered into the dim hallway, allowing him to eventually see that her pale cheeks glistened with tears. Her eyes looked enormous in her face as she gazed up at him.

"*Fuck*," he whispered savagely.

Leigh's kiss-ravaged lips parted in confusion. He braced his hands on either side of her head and pushed off the wall.

Leigh didn't move away from the wall, needing its stability, when he turned his back on her and walked out of the hallway without a word or a backward glance.

Chapter Three

෩

Later, after Leigh had taken a long shower, she shut her bedroom door and leaned against it with a growing sense of weakness and exhaustion. Only her eyes moved as she studied the room that she and Jim had always used on their visits. Sarah had decorated the mirrored vanity with a number of family pictures.

Leigh smiled tiredly as she picked up her and Jim's wedding picture. Jim looked so young and proud in it. His dark brown hair—one or two shades lighter than Tre's near-black—was slightly mussed. But it only made him look more handsome and adorable.

She recalled how he had initially requested that their posed wedding pictures be of them sitting down together, from the waist up. But she had insisted that she wanted some of him in his chair too. Leigh hadn't thought it seemed healthy for him to want to ignore that aspect of himself. When she'd expressed her concerns to him, Jim had good-naturedly agreed.

Leigh wondered now how many times Jim's amiability was just a defense mechanism to hide a depression that was growing like a cancer.

His liveliness and vivacity were what had originally drawn her to him when they were in high school. Leigh had been so reserved, so studious. She'd always been painfully aware of her family's poverty, of the name her father had made for himself as the town drunk, of her mother's reputation as the strict, sour-faced grade school nurse.

It had mortified Leigh while she was growing up to know that Doris Payton was the object of fear, dread and likely a few nightmares for more than a few sick children.

Sometimes Leigh would find herself searching her body and her soul for hints of her mother. She must have inherited something from her. Was that Doris twitching at her genes when Leigh had moments of longing for something different while she was married to Jim? Was Doris' bitterness that life had somehow wronged her ground deep into Leigh's very cells? Was that what created such bouts of melancholy in those rare, brief periods when she grieved over the fact that she would never have a child?

Leigh shook her head ruefully. No, she couldn't blame Doris for her periods of unhappiness. One of the few things for which Doris had ever demonstrated satisfaction was the fact that Leigh married into the wealthy, respectable McNeal family. Leigh hated it but the truth was that Doris saw Jim as being the perfect man—nonthreatening, kind, amenable to almost every wish that her daughter expressed.

And Jim *had* been kind. It had been perhaps his most elemental characteristic. With Jim, Leigh's self-consciousness had disappeared and she'd become more outgoing than she'd ever been in her life. She'd felt proud to be an honorary member of the McNeal family. Jeff and Sarah McNeal had created the type of home and atmosphere for which Leigh had always longed. She'd basked in their warmth and the love they gave one another so freely.

For her part, Leigh had influenced Jim into becoming more serious and disciplined with his schoolwork. It hadn't been a trivial thing to offer him. Because of his spinal cord injury Jim needed to have a deeper capacity for thoughtfulness and insight than that which was typically required of a sixteen-year-old boy.

Leigh sighed and replaced the photograph. Of course, her influence on him hadn't been great enough to win out over his depression in the last few years of his life. Feelings of guilt shadowed her awareness—familiar, hated companions.

The edges of a photo at the back of the grouping of frames caused the shadows to temporarily retreat. Leigh lifted the photograph and studied it in growing wonder.

After long seconds she remembered to breathe.

Who in the world had taken this picture? Leigh couldn't recall. Whoever had taken it had a talent for photography. What they'd caught in the image depicted far more than just solid objects frozen in a point of time.

It was a picture of Tre standing in profile next to Leigh, who was mounted on Kingmaker. Her eighteen-year-old self was smiling shyly but distractedly at whoever held the camera. Tre looked like he'd been captured in the frame by accident. The camera had caught him with his hand on the horse's flank as though he'd been steadying the regal animal. His profile tilted up toward Leigh. The expression on his face subtly spoke of pride...and longing.

Leigh ate up the image of Tre as she'd first met him. He had been twenty-three years old then, on leave from his nearly completed stint in the Navy. He'd been stationed in San Diego at the time but had returned home for a rare week-long visit. Leigh had long admired pictures of Jim's handsome brother in his uniform, heard reverent, hell-raising stories about him from his younger sibling and shared in family reminisces about the son whose rebellious, intelligent spirit had been disciplined to great advantage by the armed services.

Leigh thought that Tre looked just as handsome with his dark hair cut in a short, precision military haircut as he did with it long enough to touch his collar. The two styles just highlighted different aspects of his complex character. Her fingertip unconsciously caressed the lower portion of his photographed face.

He had been no less hard then but there was a youth and hope inherent to his features. When Leigh had been eighteen years old she hadn't been capable of seeing it. But now, as a woman who had experienced some of the happiness and sorrows of life, she recognized Tre's expression for what it was.

How had that subtle, vulnerable quality been wiped out of him? She thought of the way he'd kissed her so brutally this morning and just recently, in the hallway. Then she considered his gentleness when he'd soothed her at his house this afternoon.

No, the quality remained in Tre, no matter how elusive it may be.

Leigh would have bet money that her tears had been utterly spent. But as droplets of moisture beaded her long eyelashes, Leigh admitted to herself for the first time what she had been grieving for the past ten years.

Tre.

Her eyelids closed over the hurt that always accompanied the vivid images from her past. For once Leigh didn't run from the inevitable memories.

She let them burn her with desire and regret.

* * * * *

Ten years ago

Evening sunlight made speckled shadows and light dance together on the floor of the McNeal stable entrance. The interior was muted and dim though. A hushed, feminine croon tickled Tre's ear as he entered. Intrigued by the unexpected sound, he crossed the stable silently.

He paused, as entranced by the soft voice as his supposedly fierce horse was. He immediately recognized the young woman who leaned over Kingmaker's stall despite the fact that he'd never spoken with her in his life and seen her for all of ninety seconds just this morning as he'd been driving in from the airport to his parents' home.

Tre had paused at the side of the country road when he saw a detasseling crew and L.J., one of his parents' full-time farm hands, leaning against his pickup truck.

"What are you doing out here, L.J.? Don't tell me Dad's got you detasseling with the teenagers," Tre teased by way of greeting. L.J.'s face lit up when he saw who called out to him.

"What are you doing here so soon? I thought your dad was driving down to St. Louis to get you in the morning."

Tre grinned while he shook hands with the long-time McNeal employee and family friend. "Yeah, well I caught an early flight out. Thought I'd surprise the folks."

"Sarah will holler her head off when she sees you and then scold you for not giving her a better warning for your welcome home dinner. She's got a barbecue planned for you tomorrow night. Your dad's over on your stretch of land right now, out by the sixty mile marker, if you're looking for him."

Tre nodded his head and started to put the car into drive when a movement among the eight or nine young people who sat around the bed of an open pickup truck, drinking from water bottles and chatting during a break from the field, caught his eye.

It was July—detasseling season. Those three or so weeks during the summer when farmers hired teenagers to detassle their hybrid seed corn.

A young woman had just separated from the group and opened the driver's side door to the truck. Whoever she was she must be supervising the crew, Tre mused. He used to do the job back when he was a junior and senior in high school. The girl whipped the grimy long-sleeve shirt that she wore in order to cover her arms from the razor sharp edges of the corn leaves over her head and tossed it into the truck before she turned to say something to the younger kids.

Her long dark hair was pulled back into ponytail but strands clung damply at her neck. The fact that detasseling corn was a sweaty, dirty job didn't detract in the least from the fact that she was a remarkably beautiful woman. Tre's eyebrows rose appreciatively at the sight of ripe, firm breasts in profile before she turned and gifted L.J. and him with a view of long legs and an ass that Tre wasn't likely to forget anytime soon. Even from the distance of almost a hundred feet the image made his cock spring to life in his jeans.

When she passed out of view behind the truck Tre glanced over at L.J. wryly. Not surprisingly, the farmhand's eyes were still fixed to the site where the young woman had just disappeared.

"Guess it's clear now why you're hanging around the side of the road with a bunch of teenagers," he muttered through a half-cocked grin.

L.J. scoffed. "Come on, Tre. I know that girl's off limits."

Tre just laughed at the older man's sheepish expression, not fully understanding but already transferring his attention to the pleasant thought of surprising his mom in a few minutes.

"Hell, if she's off limits to you better lock her up while I'm here."

L.J. grinned widely. "She's not the kind of girl that you go for...or the type that always seem to flock around you for that matter. Like that blonde from Monticello a couple years back. Do you know what Tracy Sturgis told me that li'l gal said you talked her into doing behind Casey's after closing one night?"

Tre's eyes narrowed as he distractedly tried to recall what L.J. was going on about and why the hell he was fooling around with a woman in the back of a bar instead of in his bed. When a vague memory came to him, he smiled.

"*I* talked her into it? That's how the story went, huh?"

"Yeah, I guess that's why she was mooning around Casey's asking about you for weeks after the night you played patty cake with her ass—so you could talk her into a few more things," L.J. said slyly.

Tre just waved good-naturedly at L.J.'s pointed comment and shifted the car out of neutral. Still, his eyes strayed toward the group of kids as he drove past, hungry for one more glance at the dark-haired young woman.

Tre hadn't given the incident another thought for the rest of the afternoon. But he recognized her instantly when he walked into the stables later that evening. She looked like she'd showered the grime away but still was dressed similarly to how she had been when he'd seen her earlier, wearing cut-off jean shorts and a T-shirt. She stood taller than most women but she was slender and finely made. Her bare legs were long and lightly muscled. Her clothing was tight enough to grant him the view of feminine hips that curved up enticingly to a narrow waist.

He couldn't have said if her waist was overly narrow or if her hips and ass were exceptionally succulent in their roundness. He guessed that the stark contrast between the two emphasized the characteristic of the other. It was that graceful, voluptuous curve of her rear end that had made Tre instantly recognize her. A body like that wasn't something a man saw every day of his life.

Her long, thick hair was still pulled back into a ponytail that blended with the dark shadows of the stable. He fastened his gaze on her fingers as they stroked and rubbed his horse. His ears pricked into alertness just like Kingmaker's did as he focused in on the sound of her crooning voice.

"They don't know you like I do, do they, boy? You're a sweetheart down deep, aren't you, King? And you're so strong, so proud. You should have shared some of your beauty, though. How fair is it to the mares that you've got the sleekest dark-brown coat, the most velvety soft nose..."

Kingmaker whickered softly in protest when she withdrew her hand from his nose. The girl kept up her soothing banter, however, as she reached for something in the pocket of her jean shorts. When Tre realized what she was about to do the temporary trance that she'd created with her lulling voice shattered.

"Here you go, you big softy. You think you're so tough, don't you? But sugar just melts in your mouth, doesn't—"

Leigh cried out when a hard grip clamped down on her left hand, halting her motion toward Kingmaker. The same force that had stilled her spun her around so abruptly that her foot caught and she stumbled. Her eyes widened in shock when she was suddenly faced with a tall wall of muscle and a thunderous countenance.

"Who the hell are you?" Tre demanded.

Her full lower lip fell apart from its mate. The eyes that studied him were large and wary. He couldn't quite catch their color in the dimness of the stable but Tre noticed that they were fringed thickly with long, dark lashes.

"Well?" he prompted.

"Leigh," she eventually said.

Leigh recognized him after a few stunned seconds. Beyond her surprise something about the stark power of his presence, the intense vibrancy that seemed to emanate from his body in waves, had left her temporarily speechless.

"Maybe you don't value your hand much, Leigh, but I'm very particular about what King eats." Tre held her gaze and squeezed her hand in his own. "Your flesh isn't part of his diet."

"He would never bite me!" Anger made Leigh find her voice. She attempted to jerk her hand away from his but he held firm.

"No? He bit three fingers off the man that owned him over in Danville. That's why I got such a good price on him." Instead of granting her freedom, Tre brought her closer to his body by pulling on her captive wrist. He felt an unexpected desire to tame the defiance of this girl-woman.

"Jeff said that man was abusing him. Kingmaker was just defending himself," Leigh replied hotly. She flushed in anger and something else when she saw the fire that flashed into Trevor McNeal's light eyes.

"He's a valuable horse and he has the heart of a champion. He'll breed gorgeous animals with the mares I give him. But he's heartless. He could decide at any random moment that he likes your flesh more than the sugar." Tre slowly raised her hand in his own to make his point. He felt her pull downward, instinctively resisting his movements. Her tightly fisted hand made him furious.

For some ungodly reason their tense exchange was making him hornier than hell though.

L.J. was right, she wasn't his type. Her innocence practically perfumed the air. But he stood close enough to know that there was something sensual...and yes, powerfully sexual in her sweet scent as well.

He opened his hand and nodded at the fist holding the sugar.

"Give it to me," he demanded.

"*No*," Leigh muttered through clenched teeth, infuriated anew by his calm, domineering manner. "Everyone is always praising you to high heaven. They failed to mention that you were such a jerk, and a bully too, Tre McNeal."

Tre stared at her in disbelief. He had a brief, thoroughly satisfying fantasy about turning the little spitfire over his knee. How could he have ever thought she had seemed calm and impenetrable this morning?

"You've got a lot of nerve calling me names, lady, when you're the one who I just caught messing with my property. Kingmaker is spirited enough without being fed pure sugar."

"He's not just a piece of property. *You* don't deserve him."

He went still. Leigh's eyes widened with renewed wariness.

It struck her that Tre wasn't someone to be crossed lightly. She could see that he was lean, hard and in prime physical condition. He didn't look to be expending an ounce of energy in holding her while she struggled. For the first time her eyes rushed down over the length of him. Any attempts to break free of his grip suddenly ceased.

Leigh had never seen a man so virile, let alone stood so close to him that her body absorbed his heat. She swallowed with difficulty. His strong thighs and sex were distractingly obvious beneath a pair of faded jeans. Her eyes moved with cautious, growing fascination over a pair of lean hips, across a flat stomach and trim waist to a tapering torso. He wasn't muscle-bound but his strength was clearly seen in his broad shoulders and the bare, veined forearms that were lightly dusted with black hair. Leigh's eyes lingered on the v-shape that the collar of his short-sleeved shirt made on his chest. His skin looked vibrant and appealingly dark in contrast to the off-white fabric of the shirt.

When Leigh's eyes finally flickered across his hard face and met a pair of fiery eyes, a newly born uncertainty had entered her gaze.

"Like what you see?" Tre taunted softly.

Leigh's pulse throbbed rapidly in her throat. For some inexplicable reason her eyes kept dropping to his mouth. His lips were drawn into a grim line at the moment but she couldn't help but notice the shape of them...their firmness.

"Let go of my hand." She hadn't meant to whisper but all of her attention was utterly focused on him.

"When you give me the sugar."

Both of them sensed that the atmosphere of their spontaneous contest of wills had altered.

Tre waited tensely. His body had never quickened to such total arousal so quickly, and all he was doing was touching her hand. He knew that she hadn't meant her inspection of his body earlier to be sexy but that only added to the fact that it had been. In spades. He would have had to be dead not to notice how desirable she was or how firm and ripe her breasts looked beneath the clinging fabric of her T-shirt.

Silence hung heavily between them, full and potent, broken only by the occasional rustling of a horse in its stall. The scent that both of them breathed within the stable was musky and fecund.

Tre's gaze sank, slowly dragging down her neck and chest. He watched in fascination as her nipples pulled tight against the fabric of her T-shirt beneath his gaze.

Sweet Jesus. Lust pounded through the veins that fed his sex, tightening his sac almost painfully.

"Here."

Leigh's concession came in a faint whisper. Her fist opened slowly, like a pale flower. For a reason that Tre couldn't identify, the sight of her open, submissive palm holding three innocent lumps of sugar struck him as being the most erotic image he'd ever seen in his life.

"Kingmaker isn't mean or cruel. You're wrong about him," she murmured, trying to be defiant but only managing to sound dazed. Leigh licked her lower lip nervously when he just stared at her hand. Why did her body feel so tight and hot? She wondered in a flight of fancy if Tre McNeal could melt the sugar in her hand with the heat of his gaze alone. He lifted his hand to hers, passing his fingertips over her sensitive skin, tenderly removing the sugar that had begun to stick.

His dark head lowered slowly and then paused.

Leigh stopped breathing altogether when his eyes flashed to meet hers. She saw the message in them. Part of her must have recognized it, because all she did was exhale raggedly when he leaned down and tongued the residue of sweetness from her palm. The deliberate caress felt warm and slightly raspy against her sensitive skin.

She whimpered.

Tre lifted his head at the sexy sound. When he saw the heat in her eyes he dipped his head again, this time to kiss her parted lips.

Leigh moaned unevenly into his mouth as his tongue began to plunge into her depths with unapologetic hunger. Jim had kissed her many times before but it never felt like this. Tre's kiss felt like an experience her mind had never begun to imagine. His vibrant heat seemed to penetrate her until she felt fully surrounded and enfolded by his magnetic energy. Her skin felt tight and prickly when he lowered his hands to her hips and brought their bodies flush together. They groaned in unison at the pleasurable sensation of flesh against flesh.

What was wrong with her? Was it a fever that was making her hands travel up to encircle her boyfriend's brother's shoulders so desperately? Is that why she stretched back her neck so that she could experience more of his thrusting tongue and intoxicating taste?

Leigh admitted to herself that she didn't know and she didn't care.

She crushed her breasts to his hard chest, needing to alleviate the tugging, pinching pain that suddenly plagued the tips. He grunted appreciatively and roughly pulled her T-shirt from her shorts, jerking it upward high so that he could touch her. Leigh tilted her body, giving him access to her breast, needing to be touched by him as much as he apparently needed to touch her.

Tre broke their kiss abruptly at the sensation of her breast in his massaging hand. He growled low in his throat, deeply excited by her firmness, the way her breasts thrust so starkly from the plane of her chest. He shoved her T-shirt up higher and made short work of the barrier of her bra by pushing the cups downward.

He clenched his jaw tightly to try to contain his mounting lust at the sight of her high, pale, pink-tipped breasts spilling over the top of the restraining nylon.

"Tre?" Leigh whispered uneasily when she saw the hard tension on his face and he didn't move for several full seconds.

His eyes seemed to glow in the dim light when they flickered up to meet hers. Leigh was enthralled by what she saw in them before he bent to suckle at her right breast.

The sensation overwhelmed her. Leigh just stared blankly ahead, temporarily blind. She closed her thighs together tightly at the stab of painful pleasure that arrowed like lightning to her sex. He paused in the action of lashing the tight bud with his tongue when she cried out softly.

"Did it hurt?" he whispered gruffly next to her wet nipple.

Leigh glanced down. She shook her head, eyes wide.

Still holding her gaze, he reinserted the tip into his warm mouth, drawing on her until his cheeks hollowed out from the steady suction. His hand lowered to her back to keep her steady against him when she began to moan and her hips shifted restlessly.

Her flesh was sweet and incredibly responsive. He wanted…no, he *needed* to taste and touch every inch of her flawless skin. He switched his mouth to her other breast while his hand shaped and massaged the firm flesh of the other. Her hip undulations became more urgent as his focus increased.

Acting on instinct alone Tre reached between her legs and rubbed firmly through the fabric of her jean shorts.

Leigh's eyes sprang wide in shock. She hadn't realized how much tension was building in her until it broke. Pleasure tore through her. After a moment she became aware that the sharp, uneven cries that matched the spasms that shivered through her body were her own.

She blinked dazedly. Tre was holding her tightly against his heat and staring down at her.

"What-what happened?" she murmured shakily. She felt confused and disoriented, like a different person had temporarily stepped into her flesh.

Tre palmed the side of her head, sinking his fingers into her hair. He kissed her cheeks, nose and eyelids ardently. Holding her while she trembled in orgasm had made tenderness mingle with his lust.

"You came, that's what happened," he said softly next to her lips. His fingers slid next to her satiny smooth belly below her jean shorts, flicking open the first button. "Let's get these off you and we'll see what we can do about making it happen again."

"I-I don't think..."

But then his hands were pushing her shorts and underwear over her hips, returning to her ass where he massaged one plump globe greedily in his palm, and he was kissing her again with even more mind-shattering impact than before.

Even though no one had ever touched her sex before she spread her thighs without urging when his hand began to explore her. She didn't know where it was that she was suddenly desperate for Tre to touch but apparently he did. She moaned hotly into his mouth when his thumb began to make tiny circular undulations over her clitoris while his forefinger sank into her pussy. He groaned and broke their kiss abruptly.

"God you're wet, Leigh. And small. Are you a virgin?" he asked intently.

He prayed she'd say no. The thought of sinking his cock into that clinging heat made him almost wild with lust. He'd never been with a virgin before, not relishing the idea of causing anyone pain, preferring a seasoned woman who didn't go faint on him when he told her bluntly what he wanted in bed.

So he couldn't understand why he felt a surge of satisfaction when she looked at him with her huge eyes and nodded her head. A thought flashed through his brain, putting a slight chill on his desire. His fingers stilled in their pleasuring activity. He held firm even when a small cry of protest fell across her lips.

"How old are you?"

"Eighteen," she whispered.

He hesitated. "Do you want me to go on?" he asked starkly.

It was one of the many times Leigh had the opportunity to deny him. But she couldn't. Nor had she ever really had the ability to do so since she'd seen the need in his blue eyes and felt the warm rasp of his tongue on her palm.

Even before Leigh had swung her jaw in one direction, he lowered his head again to her mouth and began moving his fingers, carefully building another fire in her. He swallowed her gasps of pleasure. Leigh held onto his broad shoulders for dear life. What he was doing to her felt unimaginably good. Without ever making a decision to do so she slid her hands beneath his shirt, intoxicated by the sensation of dense muscle gloved so tightly by smooth, warm skin.

The pressure he was building in her was unbearable. She began to shift her hips restlessly, both needing his sliding, pressing, pinching fingers more than she did her next breath and also overcome by the intensity of the sensation.

"Uh-uh, honey," Tre whispered as he firmly grabbed her succulent ass and held her steady for his fingers. "Hold still for your pleasure. Don't fight it. Never fight me."

His nostrils flared and the skin on his cock pulled painfully taut as he watched her face while she came again a moment later.

Virgin or no, this woman had a rich, deep cache of sexual promise that he'd love to bring to full fruition. She was abundantly lubricating his palm with her liquid heat. He nursed her through her orgasm, carefully milking ever last tremor of pleasure out of her, held spellbound as she gave herself to him so freely and trustingly.

Tre knew that he should take her somewhere else to finish loving her. Even a rented hotel room would be preferable to making love to such a beautiful woman—a virgin, for Christ's sake—in his father's stable. But lust and need pounded unbearably into his flesh, demanding a release.

"Leigh," he rasped when she'd quieted and opened her eyes. "Have you ever touched a man before?"

"No," Leigh admitted.

Kingmaker whickered softly in the background and stamped. Her eyes widened when Tre smiled. He'd been incredibly handsome before but when he smiled he was devastating.

"I would greatly appreciate it if you would now. Don't worry, honey. I'll tell you what I want."

But Leigh was already reaching for him. Heat emanated through the denim to her fingers as she fumbled with the button fly of his jeans. Her fingertips skimmed across the hard ridge of his penis.

He groaned in agonized pleasure.

A car door could be heard slamming shut in the near vicinity. Leigh's eyes flashed up to his face. She was standing with her shorts and panties down around her ankles and her T-shirt hitched up around a bare breast. The unmistakable sound of footsteps approached the stable entrance.

Without a word Tre leaned down and pulled her shorts up to her thighs until she grabbed them. He gave her a soft shove toward a dark corner of the stable. She stumbled but regained her balance. From the inky shadows Leigh watched anxiously as he quickly fumbled with the fly of his jeans. Golden evening sunlight flooded into the stables when the door swung open.

"Tre?"

"Hey, Josh. Thanks for stopping by," Leigh heard Tre respond evenly from where she stood in the shadows, her heart pounding loudly in her ears.

She pulled at her shorts desperately in the seconds that followed. But her fears at being discovered in sexual dishevelment by a complete stranger diminished when Tre skillfully maneuvered Josh out of the stable and the door closed behind them with finality.

After she'd fastened her shorts and rearranged her bra and shirt, Leigh's legs gave way beneath her. She sank to the floor. Her body began to tremble uncontrollably.

What had she just done? Her behavior just now was so unusual for her that she literally didn't know how to make sense of it given the predictable past pattern of her life. At first her thoughts kept sliding back to the forbidden pleasure of being in Tre's arms for the last several minutes. But increasingly Jim's face popped into her mind.

And not just Jim either. Sarah's and Jeff's imagined expressions of disbelief and disgust at her behavior just now struck her with equal — perhaps greater — force.

She made a choking sound as she tried unsuccessfully to stifle her growing misery.

Chapter Four

Tre worked with focused attention on his plans for the upcoming planting season the day after his father's funeral.

At first Jeff had been skeptical about incorporating Tre's technological savvy into the upkeep of a traditional farm. But when Tre had reminded him that his father's vast acreage was worth more than most small-sized corporations, and then had demonstrated in the practical terms Jeff could appreciate how they could bring the farm business into the twenty-first century, his father had finally conceded.

For Tre's part, he liked to be able to meld the science and technology of the present with the age-old farming rituals that were ruled by the most basic laws of nature. He kept his eyes pinned on the flowchart on his computer screen as he answered the phone distractedly.

"Yep?"

"Tre?"

His eyes became more alert at the trace of worry in his mother's voice. He hit "save" on his computer.

"What's up, Mom?"

"It's Leigh. She didn't get up until ten this morning, and then as soon as she got up she said she needed to go back to bed."

Tre stood up from his desk. "What's wrong with her?"

"She says it must be the flu or something. Sore throat, body aches, runny nose. The thing of it is, I just went in to check on her. She was asleep but she's burning up."

Tre bent to pull on his boots. "I'll be over in a few minutes. I'll take her to the emergency room at Mercy."

"I already offered to do that, Tre. She insisted it wasn't necessary."

"How the hell does she know what's necessary?" Tre said irritably as he worked his free arm through the sleeve of his coat.

"Tre," Sarah admonished. "She *is* a doctor, you know."

"Yeah, and you know what they say about what kind of patients they make," Tre muttered as he paused next to the front door.

"Well, I plan to respect her wishes. That's not why I was calling. You know I usually go to bridge club on Saturday evening. I would have been happy to cancel without telling Leigh but she remembered. She insisted that I go. I'm half in agreement with her. I already missed two weekends in a row. I told myself I needed to keep up with my usual routine as much as possible now that Jeff's gone," Sarah offered with the practical level-headedness for which she was known. Only those close to her like Leigh and Tre knew how difficult it was for her right now.

"Do you think you could stay at the house for a few hours and keep an eye on Leigh? I have to admit I'm a little worried about her fever. She took Tylenol a few hours ago but she still feels so hot," Sarah continued.

"I'll be over in a few," Tre said, already moving the phone away from his ear.

"Tre, you don't have to come over yet. My bridge club doesn't even start until seven and it's only—"

Tre felt a twinge of guilt when he hit the disconnect button, but it was relatively short-lived.

Sarah was wiping off the kitchen countertops when he arrived. "I was trying to tell you I didn't need you until later," she scolded.

Tre walked toward the narrow hallway that led to Leigh's bedroom. "I didn't hear you. Did you know that it's supposed to snow tonight?"

"Oh is it? Starting when? Do you think I should cancel going to bridge club?" Sarah queried as she followed her son's looming presence down the low-ceiling hallway.

"*Tre?*" Sarah whispered savagely when she realized that Tre was reaching for Leigh's door.

"The snow isn't supposed to start until late."

"That's not what I meant. What are you doing? You can't just walk in there!" Sarah said repressively, forgetting to whisper.

Tre's brief glance told her that he could…and that he had.

Sarah watched him from the doorway as he approached Leigh's sleeping form and touched her forehead.

"Is she still hot?" Sarah whispered.

For a moment Tre didn't speak. His fingertips caressed Leigh's cheek. He waited until they were out in the hallway again before he answered.

"She still feels warm but I think the Tylenol must have started to work. It seems like a low-grade fever. She's sleeping like a rock."

"She told me that if it kept up until tomorrow she'd call in a prescription for an antibiotic. Leigh said it was likely just a virus though, and an antibiotic wouldn't do her any good. I guess she'll have to wait it out. I knew she didn't look well yesterday. She must be under a lot of stress with work.

Where are you going?" Sarah demanded when she saw her son start for the side door. She was confused by his restless, fickle behavior.

"I guess I'll salt the driveway and gas up the up the snowplow, since I'm here anyway."

"L.J. can do that," Sarah insisted. But she wasn't too surprised when Tre just shrugged and went out the door. He was like Jeff in that way, happier when he was doing something useful.

Sarah was still a little surprised Tre had acquired such a deep love of the farm and the land. He'd always been disinterested as a teenager, the exception being his lifelong love of horses. Afterward, he'd traveled around the world while he was in the Navy, and then lived in D.C. for years heading up his business. Jim'd had the promise of being the heir to the large farm when they were both young. Before his injury Jim had always been the one to trail Jeff around as his father tended to daily farm business.

Sarah shook her head. Every year of her life that passed seemed to bring something new. Sometimes those things were sad, like Jeff's death. But sometimes there were things to rejoice for too. And Tre finally settling down into a lifestyle that seemed to genuinely suit him was one of them.

If only her son could get that other matter resolved…

When Tre came in the side door an hour and a half later his mother was nowhere in sight but Leigh stood in the kitchen. She looked like a dazed wild animal caught unaware in a clearing.

His eyes scanned her as he moved closer. Her loose hair fell down her back, looking wild and very sexy. Her illness was evident in the glassy appearance of her wide green eyes, the unnatural flush of her cheeks and the pallor beneath them.

Still, Tre had to admit that he'd rarely seen her look so beautiful. His cock stirred to life of its own accord. The undesirable thought struck him that Jim had been granted the monumental privilege of seeing her like this every morning for years. The knowledge ate at him, making his stomach burn.

His eyes went inevitably to her breasts, which he knew would be bare beneath the two thin layers of her nightgown and robe. He glimpsed pale, creamy upper swells just above the pink and white satin and lace design on her bodice. The matching robe she wore cinched her narrow waist, making the fullness above it more pronounced.

She looked delicious, like a confection his tongue longed to savor.

The realization that she was ill and that he was having illicit fantasies about stripping her naked and licking every inch of her flawless skin made his temper flare.

"You shouldn't be out of bed."

"I thought I would try some tea. I don't have much of an appetite."

His mouth pulled in irritation. Tre thought he'd retrieved a measure of control when he faced her again after putting his coat on the back of a kitchen chair. He saw the expression in Leigh's fevered eyes and knew he was wrong.

Her gaze was devouring every inch of him with a hunger that easily matched his.

They both started when the teapot began to whistle.

A mixture of illness and lustful befuddlement made Leigh suddenly too sluggish for movement. Tre had the pot off the fire and was pouring water into her readied teacup before she knew what hit her.

"Where's Mom?"

"I don't know. Getting dressed for her evening out, I suppose," Leigh replied weakly.

She wanted to ask Tre what he was doing there but she found she didn't have the will to move her lips anymore. Her eyes cast woozily sideways toward one of the kitchen chairs. She needed to sit down. When she saw spots in front of her eyes one of the chants drilled in from her medical school days automatically entered her awareness.

Bend your knees and take a deep, slow breath.

The next thing she knew her face was pressed into Tre's neck and the walls were moving while she was seemingly still.

"Tre?" she asked, disoriented.

"Yes, Leigh." His voice rumbled, deep and soothing, straight through his flesh to hers. Leigh nuzzled at his warmth mindlessly.

"Why did you leave me?"

Tre stopped dead in his tracks next to Leigh's rumpled bed. A harsh comeback that would have come entirely too close to being a shout stilled on his lips when he looked down at her. Her face was averted from his gaze as she pressed her left cheek into his chest. But what he saw of her exposed skin was alarming. Her pallor seemed entirely unnatural.

That's because she just almost fainted dead away on the kitchen floor, you idiot, Tre chastised himself. His emotionally laden response to a question that was likely uttered half in delirium was put in reserve for the time being.

"I'm taking you to the hospital."

Her hair glided across his appreciative fingers when she shook her head. "No. Please, Tre. Just put me in bed. The last thing I need right now is to go for an uncomfortable car ride and then to sit for hours in the emergency room only to have some first year resident tell me exactly what I know already. It's a virus. It will pass."

Her little speech looked like it had exhausted her. She leaned back into his chest weakly. He felt her heat through his shirt and T-shirt. He hesitated.

"Promise me you won't get up again until your fever breaks then."

"Okay."

Tre couldn't help but give a small smile when he heard the watered down exasperation in her voice. She might as well have said, *"whatever, Tre"*.

He bent and settled her into the bed. A tremor shook her and he hastily drew the covers over her.

"Cold?"

In her fevered state Leigh experienced his hoarse, gentle, one-word query like a soothing caress over her achy, prickling skin. She closed her eyes and nodded. "It's just the fever. I'm at the end of the Tylenol—"

Before she could finish, Tre was going to get her more. After she'd swallowed the two pills obediently and lain back down she looked up at him. He looked extremely tall from her reclining position. His dark hair was slightly mussed and fell over his brow. Her fingers itched to reach up and touch his hard, jean-clad thighs. The capable-looking hands that hung at his sides seemed unusually hesitant, as though he wasn't quite sure what to do with them. Leigh's lips tilted at the novel idea.

"Tre?" she asked groggily.

"What?"

"You're not leaving, are you?"

"No."

Leigh clung to that single syllable as she fell into a fevered sleep.

Sarah heated them up some of the leftovers that remained from the wake. After she'd left for her bridge club Tre looked in on Leigh.

She lay in the exact same position that he'd left her in almost two hours ago. Her cheeks and lips were becomingly, albeit unhealthily, flushed from fever. A light coat of perspiration covered her face, throat and chest. Tre's face stiffened in concern when he touched her and felt her heat.

Feeling uncharacteristically helpless, he sat down carefully next to her on the bed. She moved restlessly but quickly settled back into a profound sleep.

After several moments of sitting there he noticed the picture on her bedside table. For a few seconds he didn't move.

Then he reached for the photo. Memories rushed over him. For once he didn't fight them off.

He resignedly swallowed the bitter so that he could recall the sweet.

Chapter Five
Ten years ago

ଛଠ

Jim and Tre had promised to clean up the remains of the huge Sunday morning breakfast that Sarah had prepared. Their mother was eager to get to the grocery store to do her shopping for the barbeque that she had planned for a few close friends tonight to celebrate Tre's visit home.

But neither of the young men seemed eager to get started as they lingered at the kitchen table sipping coffee and making casual fraternal small talk.

Or at least it might have been random on Jim's part. Tre on the other hand was wondering how he could get information from his little brother about Leigh without seeming too obvious. The mysterious, beautiful young woman had been gone without a trace by the time Tre had finally gotten rid of Josh Avery and returned to the stable last night. He knew about as much about her presently as he did when he'd glimpsed her yesterday at the side of the road. He was determined to find out more about her, though...and soon.

Tre realized that he hadn't been paying attention to what Jim was saying and forced himself to focus.

"She wanted me to ask you what you thought of the idea of letting her ride Kingmaker. She's gone crazy for that horse since Josh brought him over last week."

Tre made a face. "I may have broken him to saddle last year but so far only Josh and I have been able to hold him. Kingmaker's a mean son of a bitch. That's why I board him at Avery stables while I'm away. Josh is a wizard with horses. Who did you say wants to ride King?" he asked distractedly before he took a sip of coffee.

"My girlfriend. You haven't met her yet have you? You two always were missing each other when you came for those few days while I was in rehab after my accident. And during your visit last year you spent almost all of your time over in Mahomet after you bought Kingmaker. We'll both be at the University of Illinois this fall but if it weren't for her I'd never have made admission standards. Hey…"

Jim's face brightened at the sound of the front door opening. "That's her right now. We're in the kitchen, Leigh," he called out.

By the time Leigh entered the sunny kitchen, Tre's heart felt like it was somewhere in the vicinity of his right boot. When she saw him sitting at the table with Jim she paused uncertainly in the entryway.

"Hey, hon, we were just talking about you," Jim said.

Her dark green eyes flickered over to Tre. "You…were?"

"Yeah, come on in here. This is my famous brother, Tre. Tre, meet Leigh Peyton."

Leigh risked a glance at Tre. He looked every bit as intimidating as he had when he'd stopped her from giving Kingmaker his sugar yesterday. His face seemed impassive but his blue eyes glittered with emotion.

"It's nice to…nice to meet finally meet you," she managed.

"Pleasure is all mine," he drawled with subtle mockery.

Leigh sat down stiffly at the table, no longer sure if her legs would hold her.

"I was just telling Tre how much you wanted to try to ride Kingmaker."

Her cheeks burned. It was true that until last evening learning to ride King had been an obsession with her. She'd fallen flat in love with the majestic, temperamental horse. But now…

"Oh well, I'm sure he's really busy and—"

"Kingmaker's a demon. He's thrown men much bigger, stronger and more experienced than you. What makes you think you could hold him?"

Her temper was pricked before she realized that Tre was being purposefully provocative.

"He is *not* a demon," she stated flatly.

"Says who? You?" Tre asked with a patronizing grin that made her temper flare even higher.

"Maybe part of the reason Kingmaker is acting out is because you expect it of him."

Tre chuckled and glanced over at Jim. "What, your girlfriend is an animal psychologist too?"

A vague expression of surprise and confusion shadowed Jim's handsome face at the obvious hostility between two people whom he usually considered to be so pleasant and easygoing. He laughed uncomfortably. "No but she is a good rider. She used to ride Anna Jean years back but after my accident she started riding Cowboy. She's got the magic touch when it comes to animals."

Leigh's pulse felt like it would pop out of her throat when Tre's piercing eyes flickered over her with amusement. "Kingmaker is no Cowboy. He's not a nice horse and no amount of sugar or sweet-talk is going to make him into one."

"Well you should know, I suppose. Look at the wonders you've worked so far with him, right?" she goaded softly.

Tre blinked. Leigh Peyton had a backbone of steel under that soft body and calm demeanor. Despite the fact that he was furious at her at that moment he grudgingly added a healthy dose of respect to his estimation of her.

"I'm only here for a week. It's not enough time."

"I'm available every afternoon and evening once I'm done with the detasseling crew," she replied evenly despite the fact that her heart hammered madly in her ears.

"You'd have to do all of his grooming and feeding. Kingmaker needs to get used to your presence. And I won't allow you to talk to him in that..." his eyes briefly flickered over to Jim, "in a silly, condescending tone of voice. When you really want King to listen to something important he shouldn't associate your voice with coddling time."

"Fine," Leigh grated out.

Tre set down his coffee cup hard. "Fine. Be ready today at four. You can work with King a little bit before the barbecue tonight."

Jim laughed shortly when Tre stood up and started briskly clearing the table.

"Well I guess that's all settled," he muttered under his breath, although his expression said that he clearly hadn't a clue as to what it was, exactly, that had just occurred right before his very eyes.

* * * * *

"You knew perfectly well who I was when you let me kiss you yesterday in the stable. At one point, exactly, were you planning on telling me that you're my little brother's girl?"

Leigh froze in her tracks. Tre's voice resounded harshly from the shadows just behind her. She'd managed to avoid him at the barbecue held in his honor all evening but he'd apparently spotted her stealthily leaving the crowded patio at the back of the McNeal house just now. She'd almost reached the stable, where she'd planned to go to visit King and try to calm her chaotic nerves.

Leigh didn't turn around in the darkness but she didn't need to see Tre to perfectly sense the almost palpable waves of tension and anger that rolled off his body.

"I'm sorry," she said. Between the two of them Leigh was the one who had betrayed Jim knowingly. She'd actually meant to apologize to Tre this morning or this afternoon, while they'd worked with King, but Jim had been there both times.

Besides, Tre kept pricking her temper...seemingly effortlessly.

"Things got out of hand so quickly." She turned hesitantly. The muted sounds of the partygoers filtered through the humid summer night. "Are you going to tell Jim about it?"

"Maybe I should. He has the right to know, don't you think?"

Her anger flared again but sluggishly. Fatigue assailed her as well. Her constant state of nervousness and tension couldn't possibly be maintained forever. The weight of what had occurred yesterday pressed heavily on her spirit. Without another word she turned and began walking briskly to her car.

She'd call Jim when she got home and tell him she'd felt ill. That is, if it even mattered. Maybe Tre would have informed his little brother by that point about the true wanton, indiscriminant nature of his soft-spoken, innocent-seeming girlfriend.

"Where the hell do you think you're going?" Tre asked as he caught her arm, halting her abruptly.

"I'm leaving. If you want to tell Jim what happened, go ahead. There's nothing I can do about it. I'm not going to just stand here while you try to emotionally blackmail me, Tre," she said in a burst of fury.

"Be quiet, for Christ's sake," Tre muttered. "Come here."

"No, I—"

"Come here, Leigh. You owe me an explanation."

He dragged her alongside him. Several of the horses' heads came up at their entrance but for once Tre ignored them as he herded Leigh over to an empty, swept stall. The stables were dark but a dim light shone over the back entrance. It cast enough of a soft glow to allow him to see how huge Leigh's eyes looked in her pale face.

She wore her hair down tonight. He hadn't been able to keep his eyes off the glorious spill of it all evening at the barbecue. It was longer than he'd imagined before, falling in soft waves past her full breasts. Part of him felt like shaking her in frustration while another part longed to run his fingers through the dark, silky cloud.

"How long have you and Jim been seeing each other?" he began grimly.

"Two years," Leigh answered after a moment. Tre crossed his arms over his chest. Despite herself her eyes dropped down over the front of him. He looked too handsome for his own good wearing a blue cotton shirt that set off both his brilliant eyes and his healthy tan. He'd been equally devastating this afternoon wearing a plain white T-shirt that had been damp with perspiration by the time they were done working outside with Kingmaker.

"You must have started seeing him only a short while before the accident."

Leigh glanced away from him, suddenly conscious of the way she'd been staring at him. "Five months before the accident."

Neither of them spoke for a few seconds. Tre felt his irritation rise when she refused to meet his gaze.

"Do you make a habit of cheating on him?"

She did an about-face and started to walk away again. He caught her shoulder and tried to spin her around to face him but this time she was prepared to resist him. Her elbow swung wide, nearly catching his left eye. He muttered a curse and reached around to restrain her, pressing the length of her back against his chest.

"Why don't you just leave me alone, Tre?" Leigh asked brokenly as she struggled to release herself from his binding arms.

"Maybe I can't," he answered hoarsely near her ear as he bent over her. For some reason he didn't just need to feel Leigh Peyton melt under his touch again, he absolutely required it. "Not until we finish what we started here yesterday."

Leigh moaned in anguish when she felt him press his hot mouth to her ear. The deliberate yet languorous movements of his lips created an electrifying reaction in her that zipped directly down to her sex. He nuzzled her hair aside and kissed and nibbled at the sensitive skin at the side of her neck. She shivered at the pleasurable sensation.

"*Stop* it," she whispered desperately. But she'd gone utterly still in his arms and despite her words her head unconsciously tilted to the side, granting his mouth more access to her bare skin.

"No," he muttered against the fragrant skin at her nape. Her scent drove him wild. He pressed her closer into him, groaning deeply at the sensation of her ass curving tightly against his crotch.

"God you feel so good. Kiss me, Leigh."

Leigh's chin tilted up. She hadn't turned in order to kiss him, as he requested, but to see if his expression matched the naked need in his tone. But the result was the same. Because when she saw the focused, unrestrained desire in his fiery eyes she strained up to meet his descending mouth anyway.

At the touch of Leigh's soft, eager lips a red fog of lust suffused every cell of his being. Her singular taste fueled his desire, as did the sensation of her supple, firm body as he ran his hands over her. She arched back into him when he caressed her breasts. His hands lowered to greedily explore the narrow indentation of her waist and the delightful roundness of her hips.

He nipped at her damp, swollen lips hungrily a minute later as he rapidly unbuttoned her jeans.

"I have to have you." He sank his tongue between her parted lips again hungrily when she gazed up at him with desire-darkened eyes. "I won't take your virginity here in a barn, but...ah, God..." he gritted his teeth in genuine anguish as he ran one hand over the bare flesh of her ass and then between her legs. He sank his middle finger into her pussy.

Their mouths hung open only an inch apart from each other as he began to draw in and out of her gently but firmly. She clung tightly even to that narrow invader but he moved in her without the slightest friction thanks to her abundant warm cream. He watched as her lovely face tightened with arousal at his ministrations. He sank his finger one more time into her clasping heat before he muttered an apology and withdrew so that he could attack his own jeans.

A strangled sound of mixed distress and arousal filtered out of Leigh's throat when Tre shoved his jeans around his thighs and pressed his penis between the globes of her bottom. A hot, throbbing column of flesh pressed tightly against her.

"Shhh, I'm not going to hurt you, Leigh," he whispered soothingly against her ear.

His fingers found their way back to the delicate folds of her sex. God she was wet. The evidence of her reciprocal desire for him nearly sent him over the edge. The image of bending her over the stall and working his cock into her sleek little pussy nearly erased whatever residue of rationality that remained in his brain.

He dropped his head and inhaled the fresh, sweet fragrance of her hair, trying to gather the fraying ends of his control. As he did so, he found the swollen, nerve-packed, precious piece of flesh nestled in her cleft and began to stimulate her.

She whimpered and began to shift her hips restlessly. Tre gritted his teeth in sexual agony. As he pleasured her, her squirming hips unintentionally massaged his appreciative cock where he nestled in the sweet valley between her ass cheeks. His fingers increased their tempo as he kissed her neck hotly.

Tre may have thought her increasingly erratic hip undulations against his cock weren't intentional but Leigh knew better. The feeling of Tre's heavy, dense flesh nestled in the crack of her ass drove her increasingly wild. Just before the tall, intimidating wave of climax crashed into her she grew bold enough to bend her knees up and down rapidly, stroking his cock vertically in the deep cleft.

Tre's eyes crossed at the sensation. To make matters worse, she began to cry out and tremble with release. Molten heat surged against his palm. A red haze of lust filtered over his line of sight. He managed to hold out long enough to stroke her silky wet flesh until her tremors began to fade...but barely.

Then he pushed her forward until she bent over for him. He wedged his aching cock further into the furrow of her ass. He used both hands to mold the firm globes of her cheeks around his throbbing penis. His hips thrust deeply again and again. When the red haze had faded, along with the last vestiges of his barely attenuated howl of completion, Tre slowly opened his eyes.

He stared down dazedly at the erotic sight of his cock buried between Leigh's cheeks. Her pale, round flesh glistened with a record-breaking amount of his quickly cooling cum. Tre blinked, knowing he should do something but totally held prisoner by the powerful image. When he felt his cock quicken despite his mind-altering orgasm just seconds before he was galvanized into action.

Christ, all that cum...what had he been thinking? What if some of it leaked down to her pussy? Things were bad enough without him getting his paraplegic brother's eighteen-year-old virgin girlfriend pregnant to boot.

The thought made his eyes widen slightly in mild panic. Emotion gripped at his throat in a surprisingly powerful chokehold.

"Don't...don't move, Leigh," he muttered gruffly as he shrugged out of his shirt.

Neither of them spoke as he used his shirt to mop up the wetness. He felt her growing tension as he carefully dried her. When she tried to rise once, making a tiny sound of distress that tore at his consciousness, he halted her with a forearm at her lower back.

"Just a second, Leigh," he whispered.

The moment he released her she reached for her jeans and straightened. He followed suit mechanically, instinctively knowing that if she was that uncomfortable with him seeing her with her pants down at that moment, things wouldn't be made any better by him leaving his own around his knees.

Leigh was too humiliated to look at him in the seconds after she fastened the last button on her jeans. Instead she just shook her head once in rising self-mortification and turned to go. This time his hands didn't stop her but the sound of the break in his deep voice did.

"Leigh…wait."

She stopped but she couldn't bring herself to turn around.

"I'm-I'm sorry about what I said about you making a habit of cheating on Jim. I don't really think that. I was just… Christ, I don't know what I think."

He waited tensely. She eventually turned her head partially over her shoulder. Her dark green eyes glistened with unshed tears.

How could she express to him that she hadn't a clue as to what came over her when she was in his presence without sounding like a liar or a slack-jawed hick or both?

"Think whatever you want of me, Tre. You probably will anyway. I can't stop you. If there's one thing I want you to know though, it's this—I don't want to hurt Jim."

"Do you think I do?"

"No. I know you don't," she replied in a low voice.

"You're saying this can't happen again between us, right?"

She nodded decisively. "Yes."

Tre just studied her for a long second. Her cheeks were still flushed from her orgasm. Her eyes looked as wide and soft as a doe's. He opened his mouth to agree with her but instead…

"Somehow I don't think it's going to be all that cut and dry, Leigh."

Tre didn't expect the fear that flickered across her features. For a few seconds he was sure she was going to speak but then she turned and hurried out of the stable.

* * * * *

Tre felt his misery like a weight that had been applied equally to his muscles as well as his spirit as he waited for Jim in the waiting room of the doctor's office two days later. Emotions warred in him. One second he felt like bolting up and leaving not only Jim behind but the farm, his parents…Leigh.

The next he felt contrite and guilty. He loved his little brother. Jim rarely asked anything of him. Tre had longed to do whatever he could for him after his accident and during his recovery. He would have given his own legs for Jim if it was feasible, and counted himself lucky that he'd had something concrete to offer instead of feeling so helpless. Surely he wasn't so shallow as to turn him down the one time that Jim expressed the need for some fraternal support. A desperate, caged expression crossed Tre's expression as he tossed an unread magazine on the waiting room table.

But why had Jim had to ask *this* of him, of all things?

Tre's mind went back to the day before yesterday, when Jim had made his request.

In retrospect Tre suspected it had been his own fault for being so masochistic and asking Jim questions about his and Leigh's relationship. He and his brother had been watching Leigh working with Kingmaker in a corral on Grandpa's farm. She had done exactly as Tre had instructed her for the last two evenings. Tre thought she might bristle at his firm instructions after what had happened between them on the night of the barbeque, or complain when he didn't allow her to ride Kingmaker immediately. But she hadn't, and Tre was starting to gain respect for her quiet steadfastness, not to mention her obvious natural talent in dealing with the spirited animal.

Other than their business-like, terse communications while dealing with Kingmaker though, Leigh and he hadn't uttered a meaningful word to each other in two days. That fact was making Tre tenser than a new recruit on his first night spent in enemy territory.

Currently she was walking next to Kingmaker, who was in a bit and bridle. It was no easy task for such a slender female to handle the enormous fiery animal when he planted his feet stubbornly or pranced impatiently. But she was doing it admirably. Jim muttered a low curse when King abruptly tried to bolt but Leigh stopped him with a hard elbow in the groove of the horse's shoulder.

"Damn. Did you teach her to do that?" Jim asked, obviously impressed. He wiped the sweat from his brow. The evening had brought little coolness with it, especially here in the sun where they watched Leigh and King in the pasture. Jim had shed his T-shirt a half hour ago, revealing a deeply tanned torso that was hardened and muscled from two years of wheeling.

Tre shook his head but his gaze never moved from Leigh and his horse. "Nah, you were right. She's a natural. Seems she always knows exactly when to be soft with that animal and when to be hard."

Jim laughed. His youthful, handsome face looked proud at Tre's compliment of his girl. "Yeah, plus she's a whiz at anatomy and stuff. If it weren't for her I would have flunked advanced biology. If anyone would know where to apply a minimum amount of pressure for the maximum effect, it's Leigh."

The subtle inflection that tinged Jim's words made Tre's gaze flick over to him. "You sound like you have firsthand knowledge of that particular talent."

Jim smiled self-consciously and shook his head. "She does have a nice touch," was all he said.

Tre propped his foot onto the lower rung of the fence in a seemingly negligent gesture. He was shocked at how bitter the taste was that rose in his throat when he thought of Leigh's sensitive hands touching his brother's body.

"You two must be pretty close, huh?" he asked abruptly to stop his tortuous train of thought, knowing full well he was just punishing himself further.

"We've dated since before the accident."

Tre kept his profile to his brother but he nodded knowingly. "So that's why you were so eager to ask the doctor all those questions about sex back when you were in rehab."

Jim reddened beneath his tan. "Well, yeah, but it wasn't like… It wasn't like Leigh and I had ever…you know. We're both still virgins." His tone became a little defensive. "It's one of the most common questions that people have after a spinal cord injury, Tre. Think about it. Wouldn't you have wanted to know, if it were you?"

"Hell yes," Tre stated matter-of-factly, his gaze still on Leigh.

For a moment neither of them spoke as they watched her calmly lean her weight into Kingmaker when he frisked, forcing him to feel her presence. For a stretch of almost a minute the horse moved smoothly and proudly by Leigh's side.

"I really appreciated the way you talked to my doctor back then, Tre," Jim said in a hushed voice. "I was too uncomfortable to bring it up and I couldn't ask Mom and Dad to do it…"

Tre looked vaguely irritated. "What are brothers for, right? I was glad to help out in any way I could. Damn doctor should have addressed it with you immediately as far as I'm concerned."

Jim laughed humorously. "It's not like the answer was anything I wanted to hear, right?"

Tre tensed. His own sexuality was so basic to him, as natural a part of his functioning as breathing or his heartbeat. He knew very well that Jim wasn't any less of a person because he didn't have sensation from his lower chest downward. Tre knew it just as well as he knew that the last thing his brother needed was pity for that particular loss of functioning. He'd have beaten the hell out of anyone who dared to suggest otherwise to Jim.

Still, Tre was a human male, with all of the fears and insecurities that accompany that identity. By now he understood that he held the inevitable prejudice ingrained into every man on the planet since childhood. Like most men, his sexuality had unconsciously become equated with his cock.

Tre agreed wholeheartedly with the psychologist on the rehabilitation unit who had educated Jim and him two years ago. Of course sexuality wasn't just about penetration and orgasm. He rationally knew that, and he knew it from experience with the occasional female with whom he'd wanted more than just sexual gratification.

But he still struggled with his culturally ingrained attitudes. The thought of impotency was bad enough but to have no sensation whatsoever? What he knew logically warred with his primitive fears, creating a sense of anxiety that he never let his brother witness.

And now Leigh stood between them, making matters infinitely more complicated.

Jim cleared his throat uncomfortably. "It's funny that we should be talking about this, Tre. There's been something that I was hoping you could help me with, while you're here."

"Name it, Jim."

"Remember that the doctor said that when I was ready there was a drug that could help me, you know...get an erection?"

Tre's face went completely blank.

His gaze shot automatically to Leigh. Sweat glistened on the flawless skin of her arms, chest and face. When she lifted her right arm over King's neck Tre saw the clear delineations of lean, strong muscle. For a moment he compared Kingmaker's massive, powerful structure to Leigh's. She was all smooth, slender elegance. But he'd seen Leigh exhibit surprising strength on several occasions, and not just from her body, from her spirit too.

Tre knew that was why he'd agreed to let her work with Kingmaker. He'd sensed her inner strength from the beginning. He undoubtedly had guessed that King would sense it too. And he'd been right.

He watched, his heart hammering, as the young woman who his flaming spirit thirsted for like a deep chalice of cool water brought his half wild horse to a smooth, haughty walk.

"I remember, Jim," he conceded after a moment. If he had been the older brother that he should have been he would have prompted Jim with a leading question that showed his comfort level with the topic. As it was, Tre was totally aware that his brother struggled in the silence that followed.

"Well, it's just that…I think Leigh and I…we're—"

"Leigh told you that she wants to have intercourse?"

Jim paused at the lash-like intensity of his brother's voice. "No, not specifically. But I mean, we've been together now for two years." He laughed uncomfortably. "I'm going to be in college in the fall. There can't be many guys who are virgins when they start college, for Christ's sake."

Tre's jaw clenched tightly at the vulnerability in Jim's voice. "You'd be surprised, Jim. Besides…don't you remember what the psychologist told us at the rehabilitation unit? Sex isn't just about that. Even if you take a pill that makes you hard what's it going to mean to you? You won't be able to—"

"I know," Jim said with surprising harshness. "I won't be able to feel what it's like being inside of Leigh. I won't be able to come inside of her. All of my spinal nerves have been severed to that part of my body. But those medicines can bring me to life...for her. I'll be able to watch her, imagine what she's feeling. I'll know that I'm bringing her pleasure. That will be enough for me, Tre...it *has* to be enough."

Tre stared out at the pasture sightlessly.

"There are a lot of different ways to make love, Jim," Tre said stiffly after a moment. He didn't like to think of his brother and Leigh engaging in any of those ways but fair was fair, right?

"Yeah. And I think Leigh likes it...touching and stuff. It's not as if she's complaining or anything, Tre. But she's young. She doesn't have anything for comparison. I was the first guy that she ever really dated seriously. At some point she's going to realize what she's missing—"

Jim's voice broke.

Tre kept his face averted from his brother. He resignedly lowered his eyes from the tantalizing vision of Leigh too.

"What can I help you with, Jim?" he finally asked

"I've made an appointment for tomorrow to talk to my old physiatrist, Dr. Conway. He'll prescribe me the medicine I need if I ask him. I don't require you to speak for me, Tre. I'm not a sixteen-year-old kid anymore. But I could use some moral support. Do you think you could go with me to the appointment tomorrow afternoon?"

Tre swallowed the lump of gravel in his throat. "Of course."

What the hell else could he say?

What the hell else? Tre repeated to himself acidly two days later as Jim wheeled himself out of the doctor's office. A dull ache began in the vicinity of his chest when he saw his brother's smile.

What man didn't deserve a cocky grin once in awhile?

But even as Tre applauded his brother, some part of him already must have been planning to betray him.

Chapter Six

ॐ

"Son of a bitch."

Tre realized that he was speaking out loud when he saw Leigh move feverishly in her sleep. He glanced up in concern when he saw her eyelids flutter, as though she were trying to lift them while a heavy weight rested on them. The weight won out. One satin-encased arm flung forward, bringing the sheet down over her torso.

He hadn't removed her robe earlier and it was gaping open now. Tre stared, the photo in his hand and his livid self-recriminations temporarily forgotten.

She'd shifted onto her side. The shape of her breasts beneath the fitted bodice of her thin nightgown was fully revealed to his gaze. Firm, creamy curves pressed together above the low neckline, creating an enticing view of deep cleavage. The shape and color of her nipples was clearly displayed beneath the shear satin. The areolas were in a full, relaxed state due to the fever that punished her body. But even as Tre watched, a shiver convulsed her. Her nipples instantly puckered into hard, pointed crests.

"*Shit*," Tre muttered as he stared with unwavering focus. He'd have been lying through his teeth if he claimed that thoughts of reaching out and skimming the pad of his forefinger over those pale, firm swells didn't swamp his brain at that moment. When another tremor racked her slender body his lust moved quickly to the back burner. But his one-word curse still seemed to concisely sum up the whole situation for Tre.

He set the picture frame on the table at the same time he placed his entire hand over Leigh's exposed neck.

She was on fire.

Tre was on the phone with the McNeal family doctor within sixty seconds. Dr. Ambrose's wife Lucille answered. She kept her chitchat with Tre to a minimum, undoubtedly used to receiving phone calls from panicked family members at all hours of the day and night.

Dr. Ambrose told Tre to take Leigh's temperature then call him back immediately. Tre was comforted a little by the fact that Dr. Ambrose had cared for Leigh during her childhood and adolescent years.

"Leigh doesn't get sick often but whenever she does she doesn't do it halfway," Doc Ambrose had said before Tre hung up the phone. "She used to spike some exceptionally high fevers."

He had difficulty fully rousing Leigh so that he could get the thermometer in her mouth. She finally woke enough to hold the thermometer steadily under her tongue for the required amount of time before she instantly fell back into a stupor.

Tre scowled when he saw the results. He fully expected Dr. Ambrose to tell him to get Leigh to the emergency room immediately but the older man told him to try another plan of action first. He advised adding ibuprofen to the Tylenol dosage she'd been taking and told Tre to give it to her immediately, before the four-hour time limit expired.

"Isn't that going to hurt her to take that much medicine together, Doc?"

"No. It's true that you shouldn't under normal circumstances. But she'll be fine as long as you don't give her too many successive doses like that. That high fever will do her more harm if it doesn't break sometime soon. And try one other thing."

Tre remained so quiet after Dr. Ambrose told him what to do for Leigh that the doctor asked, "Are you there, Tre?"

"Yeah."

"Call me in an hour. If her fever hasn't broken by then you'll have to take her into Mercy. I hope for both of your sakes you won't have to though. The wind has really picked up and we're supposed to get dumped on later tonight with snow. Leigh shouldn't be out in this weather if we can at all prevent it."

Tre agreed and hung up the phone. He hesitated for only a second before he woke Leigh, this time more forcefully than he had when he took her temperature.

"Don't go back to sleep, Leigh," he commanded when she opened her eyes narrowly then almost immediately closed them again. Tre gripped her firmly beneath her armpits and scooted her into a sitting position. He leaned the dead weight of her upper body against his forearm as he fluffed her pillows against the headboard. She inspected him dazedly through sleepy eyelids.

"Tre?" she mouthed his name without making a sound.

"It's me. Here, take this." He held the pills against her lips. Tre saw her eyes lower sluggishly to his hand. For a second he thought she was going to question him but then she opened her mouth and accepted the medicine. When she took a sip of water to swallow them, she winced.

"Throat hurts," she managed in a raspy whisper. "What's my temperature?"

"A hundred and four plus. I spoke with Dr. Ambrose and he said you have a tendency to spike high fevers when you get sick."

"Doc Ambrose?" Leigh attempted a grin but her teeth were clattering together as if she were freezing. She shuddered violently as her body tried to throw off the unnatural heat. "How's he doing?"

Tre gritted his teeth. "*He's* doing fine, Leigh. You're the one that's about to set this bed on fire with your fever. Doc says I have to put you in a tepid bath."

Leigh's eyes rolled up to look at him at that statement but she had to blink several times to bring him into focus. "Oh. He's trying to break the fever, huh?" She flung her right leg over the side of the bed. "Okay, I'll go get in the bath," she mumbled hoarsely.

"The hell you will," Tre said through tensed lips. He firmly pushed her back against the pillows. "You're as weak as a newborn colt. Did you forget that you almost passed out in the kitchen a while ago? Just stay there, lady. If you try to get up I'll make you pay for it when you feel better, do you understand?"

Leigh opened her mouth, not particularly caring for the pointed threat in his voice, but her reply was stilled on her tongue when Tre's chin rose slightly in an unspoken challenge. She realized she was too exhausted to argue with him so she just nodded once.

"Good. I'll go fill up the tub and be back to get you in a minute," Tre said with vague contrition. He didn't like shouting at her when she was so vulnerable, but he didn't think he could take any of her sass right now either.

As the tub filled he returned to Leigh's room and asked her if she had anything fresh to change into after the bath. Leigh answered with a weak gesture at the bureau. Tre chose a pair of sweatpants and a T-shirt that seemed like they'd be a hell of a lot less sexy than the nightgown that she currently wore. He clenched his teeth when he opened up her top drawer and was confronted with several pairs of lacy panties and matching bras. He fingered the delicate fabric, finally choosing a pair of white cotton briefs that seemed to be the most innocent choice.

After he'd set her things in the downstairs bathroom and checked the temperature of the water, he returned for her.

Leigh didn't speak as he leaned over her and lifted her from the bed but her hands reached around his neck in a gesture of compliance. He set her down on the toilet when they reached the bathroom. The unnatural color that had been in her cheeks for the past few hours vanished, leaving her looking eerily pale. When Tre started to straighten she swayed. Her hands came up sluggishly to grab him but Tre was already there, steadying her.

"Okay?" he asked tensely.

"I'm dizzy. It's a little embarrassing but I think I'm going to throw up."

"Hell, that's not embarrassing," Tre assured her. He stood her up and turned her slowly, sensitive to her dizziness. He pressed her back into the full length of his body and lowered himself until they both kneeled on the tile floor in front of the toilet. Tre's right hand steadied her just beneath her breasts while he raised the lid.

For several seconds they stayed positioned like that. She didn't lean forward but her neck bent like a limp reed. Tre could easily sense her weakness and her hesitation. He leaned down and spoke quietly next to her ear.

"It's okay, Leigh."

Leigh shook her head desperately. "It's not just because it's embarrassing. I'm trying to keep it down. I need to…for the fever," she managed to get out around a gagging sound.

"Oh, right." Tre immediately saw the truth of her words. The pills she had swallowed were still in her stomach. Undoubtedly, they were responsible for her wave of nausea.

She looked completely miserable. He instinctively began to gently massage her flat belly. When she didn't protest but subtly moved back into his arms, he continued. Neither of them spoke for a minute or more while Leigh waged an inner war against the nausea. After a while Tre became aware that she was relaxing slightly.

"That feels good," Leigh murmured hoarsely, referring to his massaging fingers.

Tre leaned over to catch her words and pressed his mouth into the soft juncture of her neck and shoulder. He wasn't fully aware of his intention to kiss her but Leigh felt the caress with every cell of her fevered body.

"Do you still think you're going to be sick?" he asked when he realized that he was mouthing her neck with a mixture of contentment and hunger.

Leigh swallowed down another wave of nausea but this one was considerably less powerful than the former ones. She shook her head, not trusting her voice.

"Then we should try to get you into the tub. You're burning up, honey."

"Okay," Leigh agreed. But for several moments neither of them moved.

A shiver racked her body when Tre reached up to untie the already loosened belt of her robe but Leigh couldn't have sworn the tremor was entirely caused by her fever. She obligingly straightened her arms when he slid the robe over her shoulders. He moved temporarily away from her and the satin material fell between their bodies and shimmered onto her bare calves.

When she felt his fingers enclose the thin strap of her nightgown at her shoulder, her hand covered his. She made a small sound of protest.

"It's all right, Leigh. Despite the way I acted yesterday I'm not that much of a jerk. I'm not going to take advantage of you while you're sick like this."

But after Leigh removed the restraint of her hand and Tre swept the straps off her creamy shoulders, he wondered if he truly had it in him to strip Leigh naked and touch her in an objective, detached manner.

His expression turned wooden as he lowered her nightgown over her waist and then her hips. He refused to glance over her shoulder at her bare breasts, although he could have — he was a good nine inches taller than her. But the sight of her elegant, pale bare back, the delicate line of her backbone and the beautiful curve of her hips as they narrowed to a slender waist were trying enough.

He paused indecisively when he saw the twin dimples at her lower back but then pushed down the soft material with a matter-of-fact briskness he was far from feeling. Knowing he couldn't keep hesitating when her health was at stake, Tre hooked his fingers into her underwear and dragged those down her thighs along with her nightgown. He moved jerkily when he caught a glimpse of her pale, naked bottom.

Christ, he loved Leigh's ass. Some things never changed.

Leigh gave a muffled sound of distress when Tre stood quickly, bringing her with him.

"Sorry," he mumbled stiffly, ashamed of his abruptness. He leaned over and helped Leigh step out of her nightgown and panties with far more patience. Or maybe he was just enjoying bending over her bare butt and fitting himself to her. The thought made him back away rapidly.

"Can you step in if I hold you?" he asked her in a voice that didn't sound like his own.

Leigh nodded but Tre thought she looked like she was at the end of her rope. Her foot caught at the edge of the tub but Tre held her steady with a muffled curse. She was more cautious with her second foot.

"*Slowly*," Tre instructed tersely as she lowered herself to the tub while he held her waist firmly. Her saw her gritting her teeth as though she were in pain as the water inched up her pebbled flesh. She gasped loudly when she finally sat and the water lapped around her belly and waist.

"It's freezing, Tre McNeal!" she shrieked. Her trembling amplified alarmingly. "What are you trying to do, kill me?"

Tre's anxiety found an outlet in a sharp burst of laughter. It took a moment for it to sink in to his awareness that submersion in the cool water in her fevered state was magnifying Leigh's discomfort to the point of acute pain. Energy seemed to surge through her. She tilted on one hip, brought her feet beneath her and reached for the side of the tub. Water sloshed up and splashed Tre.

When he realized what she was doing he increased the pressure of his hold on her waist and pressed downward. The strength with which she pushed desperately on the side of the tub shocked him.

"Hold *still*," he ordered.

Her usually soft, smooth skin roughened with thousands of goose bumps as her body tried to increase its surface area to throw off the unwanted heat. "Stop flailing around, damn it. I'm not kidding, Leigh!" Tre barked out so sharply that she temporarily sagged against him. When she spoke he could hear her teeth chattering.

"It's...so cold," she cried miserably.

Tre almost loosened his hold when he saw a tear leak past her clenched eyelids. "I know it seems that way. I'm sorry. It feels cold to you because your body is so hot. Just try to relax." He tried to calm her with a soothing hand at her waist but she moaned softly.

"That hurts."

Tre immediately stopped stroking her, recognizing that her pain came from her overly sensitized skin. "I'm going to let go of you, Leigh. Are you going to stay put?"

He realized that he was staring fixedly at her tightly drawn nipples as they trembled from the shivers that racked her body. Tre resolutely turned his gaze to her face. He waited until he had her agreement then slowly removed his hands from her. Her arms remained at the sides of the tub. Her slender muscles flexed in uncomfortable tension.

"Try to relax, Leigh."

She grimaced. "It's easy...for you to...say," she accused irritably as she trembled.

"You're going to have to get down lower in the water."

"No!"

Tre's face tightened when he heard the increasing hoarseness of her voice. How could making her sit in cool water while she froze half to death help her sore throat? But even as he thought it he reminded himself that she had been far from freezing when he had just been touching her. She was burning up.

His resolve stiffened and he scooped some of the water in his palm and sluiced it onto her back. Her roughened cry almost made him pause but he hardened his heart. When he saw her arms stiffen he murmured a tense warning.

"Don't you dare, Leigh."

"I'm going to get you back for this, Tre," she breathed out with a harsh sob. She started when he splashed cold water on her again. "I think you're enjoying torturing me."

Tre made a contemptuous sound. "If it helps you to think that you go right ahead, honey."

Leigh pulled her knees inward toward her body and wrapped her arms around them. She turned her head away from Tre, resting her cheek on her knees.

Neither of them spoke for a few minutes as he continued to wet her with his palm and Leigh shivered uncontrollably. Tre thought he'd never witnessed such a bundle of pure human misery.

He felt her tremors abate momentarily when he tenderly gathered her dampening hair in one hand and sluiced water over her fevered neck.

Awareness broke through Leigh's discomfort like a few rays of sunlight in a shadowed room. She focused on the silence broken only by sound of the water trickling off of her body back into the tub. She listened to Tre's dipping hand with sharp attention and waited with anticipation for him to splash her with water...for his touch on her bare skin.

As if Tre had read her mind, he palmed her neck gently and let the water trickle down her shoulders, back and chest. Long fingers lightly massaged the tense muscles at the sides of her neck. When a tremor broke over her he removed his hand and retrieved more water. But when he opened his palm across the curve of her middle back and she didn't shudder, he lightly fanned his hand outward over her skin, dispersing the water over her in a thin, cooling sheet.

After a few more minutes of his careful ministrations Leigh sighed raggedly. Tre almost felt some of the unbearable tension that had been racking her body leave her with the exhalation. He tenderly stroked her neck and scalp.

"I think you can lean back now, honey. Your shivering has almost stopped."

Leigh hesitated but then slowly leaned back until she reclined in the tub. She gritted her teeth at the feeling of being fully submersed but Tre's patient preparation of her body made it far less painful than originally sitting in the water had been.

After a moment her body settled. She was far from comfortable but she was no longer miserable either. Leigh's eyes fluttered open when she realized that Tre hadn't spoken or touched her in many seconds. He was still kneeling by the tub. His black hair had fallen forward and brushed his dark brows.

He'd removed his outer shirt at some point and was just wearing a dark gray T-shirt. Leigh saw that she'd soaked him with water when she'd struggled. Her eyes played across his chest, shoulders and muscular arms.

"I'm sorry I got you wet," she whispered.

Tre almost glanced down at himself. But instead his eyes remained glued on her body.

She experienced his piercing gaze on her like a touch. It made her acutely aware of herself. She felt vulnerable, naked and exposed to him but she saw that she was beautiful to him as well. She read it like text in the depths of his blue eyes.

"It's okay," was all he said.

"And I'm sorry that I said you were enjoying making me miserable." She watched as his strong neck muscles convulsed as he swallowed.

"I'm no Boy Scout, Leigh. I may not have been enjoying seeing you in pain but I sure as hell enjoyed touching you."

Leigh's eyes widened when he leaned forward and braced one elbow on the tub. Their gazes held, only inches apart.

His hand dipped beneath the water with slow, sensual stealth. He palmed the underside of her breast. He searched her expression for a reaction.

When her pupils dilated and her lower lip fell away from her upper one he began to massage her, glorying in her firmness, her shape, her weight. He glanced down at her breast in his hand and brushed his thumb and forefinger over her erect peak.

"You're larger here than you used to be," he said distractedly.

Leigh stifled a cry of arousal as he lightly pinched a sensitized nipple. The fever seemed to maximize her pleasure, make it edgier—more imperative. Her nipple pulled into painful erection. Her thighs instinctively squeezed shut, tightly, to alleviate the equally unbearable throb at their juncture.

"I was only eighteen then, Tre," she managed eventually in a thready whisper as he attenuated his caress by soothing her nipple with his fingertips.

"And you're a woman now."

The way his eyes looked when they traveled over her body and then her face left Leigh in little doubt that he'd meant it as a compliment. Her fevered lips fell opened and she inhaled sharply when he transferred his hand to her other breast. He glanced down when he felt it pull tight beneath his fingertips.

"It feels good because of the fever?" Tre asked as he watched himself palm and pinch and stroke her breasts and nipples.

"It would feel good anyway," Leigh admitted. "But yes, the fever is making them more sensitive."

The roughness of her voice made him glance up sharply. She made a small sound of protest when he released her and brought his hand out of the water.

"I'm sorry, honey. I know I'm a pig, but you're beautiful." He gave a slow smile when he saw her embarrassment at being confronted with the name she'd called him yesterday. "If I could have stopped myself I would have."

"Oh." Leigh didn't know how to respond to his honesty or the rare glimpse he was allowing her to see of his soul. When Tre witnessed her stunned reaction he came to himself by slow degrees.

"Will you be okay just lying there for a minute?" he asked gruffly as he stood. "I need to get the thermometer."

Fifteen minutes later Leigh was tucked back in her bed with the covers pulled firmly around her chin. She no longer shivered but she felt weariness in every inch of her body. Tre had just left a few minutes ago after retaking her temperature to call Dr. Ambrose with the results. She struggled valiantly to keep her eyelids open.

"What'd he say?" she asked groggily a few seconds later when Tre entered her room.

"He says you're off the hook for now." He hid a grin when he saw her smug expression. "But barely, Leigh. He said I should take you to the emergency room if your temperature goes up more than two degrees during the night."

"It won't," she whispered.

Something in the way she watched him made him draw closer. He sat down next to her when she scooted over slightly on the bed, making room for him.

Tre conceded that perhaps there would always be certain barriers between them. Nevertheless, something had shifted between them in the past hour. The restriction that had stood between them from the very beginning, the one that prevented them from openly appreciating each other with their eyes without feeling anger or shame or guilt, had been irrevocably thrown down by Leigh's burning fever. When his hand rose to brush back her dark hair he realized with wonder that other prohibitions had been burned away as well.

"It's snowing outside," Tre finally murmured with rare mellowness.

"It is?" Leigh felt drowsy, content. She wanted to stay awake to fully savor Tre's rare, cherishing caress, but the same touch seemed to be beckoning her further and further away from him into sleep. She shook her head sharply, as though her sleepiness was a pesky fly that had just landed on her nose. When she saw Tre's slow smile she knew that he'd understood instinctively.

"It's okay, Leigh. Get some rest."

He continued to touch her until well after it was obvious that she was deeply asleep. He caught one shiny, dark lock between his fingers and stroked its entire length. Leigh's hair was shorter than it had been when she was eighteen years old. It currently fell several inches below her shoulders in a stylish, layered cut. With less weight on the ends her hair looked fuller and waved beguilingly. Tre loved the sensual feel of it against his fingers.

Of course, it had been beautiful when she was younger too, when it cascaded halfway down her back. Tre perfectly recalled the way it surrounded her pale face like a dark cloud when it hung loose, the near-black color of it as she'd treaded water in Grandpa's pond on that hot summer evening and gave herself to him with a generosity that still, to this day, moved his body and spirit in recollection.

Chapter Seven
Ten Years Ago

೫

Leigh's face was flushed with pride and a profound awareness of Tre as he helped her dismount from Kingmaker for the first time. It didn't fade as she watched him secure the horse to a sturdy branch. Never mind that she hadn't ridden King solo. She'd made her maiden tour in front of Tre.

Her cheeks deepened in color at the memory of sitting between his long, strong thighs. Her blush only increased when she observed him casually peel off his T-shirt.

"What are you doing?" she asked sharply.

They'd managed to keep a safe distance from each other for the past several days but the sight of Tre's naked torso hardly made her feel secure. Tre and Jim shared similar dark coloring and both of them were appealingly muscular. But Tre was taller than Jim and the long, gradual taper that led from a trim waist across a stomach too lean not to display every muscle to perfection and up to broad, powerful shoulders was a genuine tribute to God's talent as an artist.

And Tre was older than Jim. His muscles were hardened and tried from years of work and military exercise. There wasn't a trace of softness to him. The dark hair curling on his chest wasn't too excessive but it still emphasized his masculinity. When Leigh's eyes wandered down over him without a trace of her usual discipline she verified for the thousandth time what she already knew.

Tre didn't flaunt his masculine sex appeal. He didn't need to. It spoke loud and clear for itself.

Tre slowed his movements as he pulled his T-shirt down over his forearms and hands. His awareness of the young woman who stood before him seemed to thrum and vibrate with the slightest shift of her hungry eyes.

He'd reached his limit. He couldn't keep resisting her. She was like a fire in his blood. If he was about to make the biggest mistake of his life in betraying his brother, all Tre could say was that his error felt compulsory.

"I told you," he said with a forced, lighthearted tone, "I'm going swimming. Don't tell me it's not hot enough for you."

There was amusement and barely veiled desire in his blue eyes when he made a point of glancing down at the dampness that had soaked through her T-shirt between her breasts.

Leigh scoffed but her feet shifted anxiously. She may be innocent about many things but the elemental woman in her knew the danger of being trapped in a cage with a tiger. She'd already been foolish enough to be cornered with Tre two times too many. They may have managed to keep their hands off each other for the past few days but that didn't mean they weren't completely aware of each other. They'd been eyeing each other, breathing each other and engaging in an almost constant dance of sexual push and pull.

Still, the edgy tension between them had been stifled for the past few days with varying degrees of success. Until this evening, that is.

For a reason Leigh couldn't name, she sensed a new quality in Tre. He had seemed different…more intense, ever since he'd arrived back at the farm this evening following some mystery errand with Jim.

A restraint had been loosened in him. He was like a coil about to spring free. That knowledge filled her with anxiety and a growing anticipation. Leigh licked her lower lip nervously while straining to keep the conversation as even-keeled as possible.

"I'm dying of heat and you know it," she finally answered lightly. "It must still be in the nineties. You go ahead and swim and I'll keep Kingmaker company," Leigh said with only a trace of longing as she gazed out at the calm lake. She'd never been swimming in it before Jim's accident. Since his injury Jim could no longer swim and she'd never gone alone. But the idea of a cool dip in the water after such a scorcher of a summer day and all the hard work she'd done with Kingmaker sounded appealing.

Tre rubbed his bronzed, sweat-glistening, taut belly absently. "Come on, Leigh. I know you want to dive right in."

Leigh's gaze flickered automatically to the hand on his abdomen before it flew to meet his eyes. There hadn't been a subtle innuendo in his statement, had there? She frowned when she saw the glint of amusement in his eyes. Teasing she could deal with. She turned and began to loosen Kingmaker's saddle.

"You go ahead," she insisted. She threw a defiant glance over her shoulder. "My mother always told me that swimming in these country lakes was dangerous. You can get way in over your head before you even realize it."

"Sounds like something Doris Peyton would say."

Leigh glanced around sharply. It wasn't the response she'd expected from Tre. "You-you know my mother?" she asked. Embarrassment surged through her at the unintentional tremor in her voice.

Tre's expression became inscrutable. "Just *of* her. I do know your dad, Charlie, though. I've met him over at Casey's."

"Oh." Leigh examined Kingmaker's saddle as if it might hold the key to the mysteries of the universe. When Tre didn't speak or move for several seconds Leigh murmured, "My mom really hates that place."

"'Cause your dad spends so much time there?"

Leigh nodded briskly to cover her discomfort. "And because he spends so much of my mom's paycheck getting drunk there every night."

Tre's eyes never left her profile. He easily sensed her disquietude on the topic. He also guessed accurately that Leigh had been spoonfed her mother's side of the story all her life, that she knew mostly shame and anger when she considered her father.

Tre had initially only known Charlie Peyton a little, but his reputation had preceded him. He'd been surprised to discover that beneath the surface reputation of the town drunk there existed a man with no small amount of charm and the soul of a poet.

Charlie Peyton was a sad, broken man. Tre couldn't abide by his actions, especially now that he knew Leigh and guessed the effect they must have had on her. But he could tolerate Doris Peyton's behavior on the two occasions when she'd stormed into Casey's to claim her husband even less. Tre still cringed when he thought of the way the acid-tongued shrew had verbally flayed and humiliated Leigh's father in front of the only peers that he had.

His eyes sharpened on Leigh's averted face. She was the real tragedy of Doris and Charlie Peyton's dysfunction. How had two such essentially self-centered, coarse individuals created the graceful, sensitive and intelligent young woman who stood before him?

Before he was fully aware of what he was doing Tre took both of her upper arms in his hands and turned her to face them.

"You have nothing to be ashamed of, Leigh."

"I never said I was ashamed of anything!"

When she saw compassion in his expression she shrugged her shoulders roughly in an effort to rid herself of his touch. The last thing she needed from this man was pity. But Tre wouldn't let her back away.

"You didn't have to say it. I see it written all over your face and your body."

"Oh, thank you *so* much," she said in a low, sarcastic voice. "I guess they taught you how to be a psychologist in the Navy along with giving you all that technology training. Well here's a little advice, Tre—stick to the computers."

"Your mother has passed on a little of her venom, I see," he said casually.

Leigh mouth dropped open. "I'm *not* like her."

Tre tightened his grip on her arms when she tried to get away from him. He leaned over and brought her face close to his. Leigh went very still.

"I know you're not. You're very different from Charlie too. That's what I was trying to say from the very beginning, Leigh. Doris, Charlie and you are all three unique people. Sometimes circumstances and nature throw people together into a family and God only knows the logic behind it. But I can guarantee one thing—there's no reason for you to *ever* experience a trace of shame for their behavior. You should only be proud of who you've become...who you are. Even more so than most people, because everything you are is a credit to you alone."

Leigh stared at him in dawning wonder. What he'd said had touched her enough but the depth of emotion that had accompanied his communication held the true message, and that was what left her temporarily speechless.

Slowly Leigh became aware of how close they stood. She could see his steady heartbeat pulse at the side of his neck. From this distance she observed for the first time that his eyes were only a pure, uniform cerulean blue around the outer portion of his iris. Around the pupil aquamarine, green and dark blue crowded side by side like a vivid pointillist painting.

She inhaled the scent of a healthy sweat that overlaid the smell of fresh soap and the spicy aftershave that he'd likely applied after his shower this morning. Beneath all of that was the essential scent of Tre, musky, male and compelling. Her gaze lowered over his strong, proud nose and lingered on his mouth.

Tre's body tensed with desire when Leigh licked at her lower lip in a furtive, nervous gesture. The sight of her quick pink tongue and the way she was staring at his mouth caused a fire to leap high in him. The fire had been burning ever since he'd first heard her crooning to Kingmaker.

He was just having more and more difficulty banking that flame.

"Leigh, if you keep looking at me like that I'm not going to be able to stop myself from kissing you…for starters."

Leigh's eyes raced up to meet his when she took in not only what he'd said but his hard tone of voice. This time when she tried to move away from him Tre reluctantly let her go. He watched her silently as she touched her fingertips to her cheek as if she could rub away the telltale blush that suffused her skin.

"I thought we agreed this was going to stop between us," she murmured.

"I never agreed to that, Leigh."

Leigh glanced out at the lake anxiously. "What about Jim? It's wrong for us to be sneaking around his back like this."

"I know that. Believe it or not I'm not taking this lightly."

"You're not?" she asked uncertainly.

"No," he replied irritably. But then he noted the vulnerability on her face and he thought of how he'd treated her the other night—a virgin, for Christ's sake, and he'd bent her over in a stable and brought himself off in the furrow of her ass. He closed his eyes briefly in regret and unintentional renewed arousal.

"Look, I'm sorry I've been coming on so strong. But the fact of the matter is I'm very attracted to you. I won't lie and say I don't wish like hell that you weren't my little brother's girl."

When he saw the deepening expression of distress on her face he sighed. "Shit...just—just forget about it for right now. Let's just spend a little time together, okay? That's not too much to ask, is it?"

Leigh looked doubtful.

"I think what we both need is a good dunk in the cold water." His eyes sparkled with wry humor. "I won't touch you, Leigh. I promise."

Leigh hesitated. "I shouldn't. I don't have anything to wear swimming," she finally stated lamely.

She couldn't believe that she'd just been seriously considering his proposal, knowing full well what was going on between her and Tre. The concept of being this overwhelmingly attracted to a man was foreign to her. She had no map for navigation.

Talk about swimming in deep, dangerous waters.

The smart thing to do would be to leave right now. It wasn't much more than a mile back to Grandpa's house. Instead she eyed Tre speculatively. "You don't have anything to wear either. If you swim in your jeans and then get in the saddle wet you're going to—"

"Who said anything about me wearing my jeans?"

Her words stilled on her tongue. Her arms crossed over her chest defensively. "Very funny." When Tre raised his black eyebrows innocently Leigh felt a little hurt. "Stop playing with me, Tre."

Tre paused in his backward walk. "What do you mean by that? I'm not playing with you."

Leigh's chin rose. "Yes you are. You think it's funny to tease me when you know that I don't know how to respond to your...sexual innuendos."

Tre's mouth fell open in genuine surprise. "Honey, I wasn't trying to be suggestive by saying I wasn't going to wear my jeans swimming. Hell, I was just stating the truth. Jim and I have swum in this lake since we were five-year-olds and I don't think a stitch of clothing ever touched that water once."

It was Leigh's turn to look discomfited. "Oh. I see." She watched him with increasing wariness when he crossed his arms. The sight of his flexed chest muscles seemed to defy her not to glance downward. Leigh lost the dare.

"Does that mean that you thought it was sexy? The idea of me swimming naked?"

Leigh gave a sigh of mixed disgust and amusement. "You're too much, Tre McNeal. No, that isn't what I meant."

"Good."

Leigh examined him closely, surprised by his response. "*Good?*"

"I don't like it when beautiful women have sexual fantasies about me. It makes me feel so used."

Leigh snorted. "Right. I'll try to keep that in mind."

Still, she might have seriously taken her own advice instead of resorting to sarcasm when she saw the attractive, devilish grin on Tre's lips.

"Okay, now that we've settled that, you better look away until I get in the water, out of respect for my shy ways. And then I'll do the same for you."

"If you think I'm getting in that water with you naked you're crazy."

Tre rolled his eyes with exasperation. "What's the big deal? Look, if you want to leave on your T-shirt and underwear, you could. If you keep your jeans dry they should protect you on the short ride back on Kingmaker."

Tre spoke casually but he carefully measured her reaction. He could tell by the rapid, nervous flicking of her eyes that she was seriously considering doing what he suggested. Before she could get the "no" off of her tongue he prodded quietly, "Come on, Leigh. You've been doing a great job with King. You rode on his back for the first time today and survived. Don't you want to do something a little crazy to celebrate, just for once?"

His steady, warm gaze on her seemed to pull the words out of her against her will. "All right. If you promise to give me privacy when I get in and out of the water."

It was hard not to feel good about the decision when she saw the smile that lit his face. It made him look years younger and achingly appealing. To see Tre in a light, carefree mood when all she'd been the recipient of thus far was his concentrated lust, frowns and sarcasm warmed her from the inside out. She couldn't help but wonder how things would have been between them if their circumstances were different…if it weren't for Jim.

Once they were out on the dock Tre insisted that she go first, turning his back. Leigh's eyes stayed on him suspiciously as she removed her boots.

"Is it deep enough to dive?" she asked after she'd hauled off her jeans, keeping an anxious eye on Tre all the while. She only waited for his affirmation before she ran to the end of the wood pier and soared into the air.

Tre turned around when he heard the splash and the subsequent appreciative whoop that Leigh let out when she surfaced again.

"It's nice and cold down deep," she called out breathlessly. "It feels like heaven."

He smiled wide at her enthusiasm. He reached for the top button on his jeans. A laugh fell past his lips when he saw her sudden wide-eyed expression of panic and the way she turned away from him so quickly.

When he surfaced from his dive they were only feet apart. They shared a goofy smile, both instantly reverting to the ten-year-old kid that comes alive in all adults during a rare summertime swim.

"Guess you don't wear contacts, huh?" Tre asked.

Leigh shook her head in puzzlement. "No. Why?"

"Because I didn't want you to complain when I did this."

He pulled back a powerful arm and sliced his cupped palm through the water. Leigh was temporarily blinded by the wave that showered her face. She gave a yell of fury and began to splash Tre back in earnest but the sheer amount of water he could send her way with his greater strength finally overcame her and she turned and retreated. When she paused after thirty seconds of swimming she was near the middle of the lake and blessedly free of all the splashing water.

Tre saw her startled expression when he broke the water within ten feet of her. She pointed a wet finger at him repressively but a grin pulled at her pretty mouth.

"Don't you dare, Tre. You forced so much water into my eyes that I see three of you."

He laughed, vaguely contrite. "I'm sorry, how terrible for you."

The smile lingered around her lips when she shook her head. "It's not so bad," she eventually said softly.

Leigh had to remind herself to keep up the automatic motions of treading water as she watched him so earnestly. She glided closer.

He saw her smile fade as she drew nearer to him in the water and knew the precise second when her lips parted and an entranced expression came over her face. Despite an almost overwhelming urge to touch her he recalled his promise and kept his hands busy treading water.

"Do you date a lot, Tre?" Leigh murmured.

"Some," he answered. He watched avidly as Leigh bit her full lower lip.

"You must think it's kind of strange...the way I've been...acting around you," she almost whispered. "I would understand if you did. I can't understand it myself."

The water rippled around their bodies softly in the short silence that followed.

"The only thing that I think is strange about you is how much I want you. It's never felt so strong for me."

Leigh blinked heavily, thoroughly bewitched by his deep, low voice. Before rational thought could interfere she leaned forward and sipped the droplets of water from his firm lower lip.

Her kiss was butterfly soft....and sweet...so sweet. Tre held his breath as he turned his head slightly to get a better angle on her lush lips. When he pressed back he did so gently, as though she were a wild creature that could startle and flee from his presence at any moment.

Leigh's breath caught in awe. Every time he'd kissed her before it had been with a passion that nearly blinded her with its intensity. But this experience—this slow, sliding and pressing and nibbling—was wonderful too, and every bit as intoxicating.

She'd never in her wildest dreams imagined that a man could taste so good, like drinking the essence of concentrated desire. She flicked her tongue against the damp seam of his lips. A low growl resounded from his throat but he still didn't break his promise to not touch her. Leigh's eyes opened wide and she inspected his face.

His eyes leapt with blue fire as he watched her with a steady focus.

Before she could stop herself she sank her tongue into his mouth. As she shyly explored his depths and teased his tongue into dueling with her own, her hands stroked his shoulders lightly. He felt hard and warm despite the cool water that lapped around them.

Leigh pulled herself closer and deepened the kiss.

When the tips of her breasts brushed Tre's chest, taunting him, and he felt the lapping currents from her treading water swirl around his erection, he gently broke her increasingly ardent embrace. If she got any closer she was going to be pressing against his bare, straining cock and he wouldn't be able to control himself. She made a sound of protest as she tried to get closer to him.

"Honey, I...can't keep kissing...you and not touch...you back," he said gruffly against her seeking lips. Despite his words, he responded to her awakened hunger in kind, nipping at her lips between words. When she slid her hands down over his back and down his sides, he muttered a curse.

"Leigh, that's not fair, honey. We better get out."

He held her hand and pulled her with him in a graceless crawl to the shallows at the side of the dock where Jeff dumped sand every few years to make a small beach for swimmers.

Tre had made a promise to her and he meant to keep it. But Leigh was much more of a temptation than he'd ever imagined...and he'd imagined plenty. The evidence of her reciprocal desire for him was heady stuff, leaving him disoriented and intoxicated with need.

As soon as he stood, in about five feet of water, Leigh reached up for him again.

"Leigh? I thought you didn't want this," he muttered unevenly between her kisses.

"I don't...*but I do,*" she cried softly. "How could I not want it?" she wondered desperately against his damp, muscular neck. He felt and tasted like a slice of heaven. She bit gently. Tre groaned.

"I promised not to touch you," he muttered in increasing agony.

"Just let me touch you then," she whispered next to his lips. She suddenly wanted nothing more than to do just that — to run her hands and fingertips over every inch of the gorgeous male animal who stood in front of her.

Tre's lips sagged open at her impulsive statement.

She took advantage of his temporarily stunned state to shift herself onto the shallower side of the lake so that their disparity of height evened somewhat.

Tre stood very still as her hands and sensitive fingertips began a tortuous tour of his chest, sides and abdomen. The summer sun beat down on his shoulders relentlessly while Leigh just as surely enflamed the parts of his body that were submerged in the cool water.

She sighed in pleasure when she touched smooth skin covering hard, dense muscle. Her fingertips lightly detailed his spine and outlined his shoulder blades. They traveled over his flat abdomen and chest with even more urgency. When she spread her fingers and delved them into the springy hair at his chest, she felt Tre go rigid beneath her touch. She glanced up cautiously into his eyes, worried that she'd done something to displease him.

"Don't stop, Leigh," he implored huskily.

His eyelids narrowed with desire as he watched her examine him closely then allow her hands to follow the path of her eyes. Her touch was exquisite. He exhaled with pleasure when she grazed a fingernail over his nipple. Leigh's eyes flew to meet his. This time she recognized the expression on his face though, and her nail returned to lightly abrade him. Her attention turned avid as she studied the effect of her touch on his flesh.

"It feels good there?"

Tre laughed harshly. "It feels good when you touch me anywhere. But yeah, it feels especially good there."

"They're like mine?" she whispered cautiously.

Tre's eyes flickered hungrily down to her breasts, which were flagrantly on display beneath her wet T-shirt. She wasn't wearing a bra. He forced himself to look away.

"Yours are a hell of a lot prettier than mine but if you're asking if it feels good when you touch me there, the answer is hell yes," he replied thickly.

"Oh." Her sigh tickled his already aroused nipple, pulling him more erect. When she leaned forward and kissed him Tre stifled a gasp of pleasure. Her eyes immediately rose to his.

"It's good, honey. I like it," he assured her softly. Tre closed his eyes briefly to try to cool his overheated body. The sight of wide dark green eyes, both innocent and impassioned at once, was an image that would stick with him until he was an old man.

So would the sight of her dropping her head and delicately tonguing one of his hypersensitive nipples.

"Leigh," he muttered desperately. His cock bobbed enthusiastically against his abdomen, straining and unbearably tight. His promise not to touch her faded to oblivion as his fingers delved into her hair and pressed her head against him. His lust pitched into an aching pain as she licked avidly and rubbed her lips sensually against him. She pursed her lips and sucked him gently.

"Honey, if you keep that up I'm going to shame myself by coming right now when my cock never got so much as a friendly pat on the head."

She looked up at him sharply. Humor and desire gleamed in his eyes. Leigh wasn't used to illicit language. From Tre it didn't strike her as dirty though, only earthy, honest and extremely arousing. She felt a measure of gratification, despite her anxiety, when she reached down and encircled her hand below the head of his penis and his eyes sprang wide.

"Holy shit," he muttered almost incoherently.

Leigh's burst of confidence almost faded to nothing at the sensation of him in her palm. He was so thick that she couldn't fully encircle him with her hand. She moved slightly, allowing herself to feel the paradox of the hard, dense pillar gloved in smooth, taut skin.

"*Oh!*" she murmured in stunned pleasure. She wasn't unfamiliar with the anatomy of animals or humans. She'd always been gifted in science and biology. But what she held only vaguely resembled what she'd imagined a penis to be like. When he'd pressed against her and climaxed a few nights ago she'd begun to guess how flagrantly powerful he was.

Yet at the same time she acutely experienced how vulnerable this man was to her touch. She met his eyes.

"I had no idea that you'd be so beautiful," she murmured in genuine amazement.

Tre ground his teeth together hard to keep from spilling himself into her hand then and there.

"How... What do I do?" she asked. The sight of her uncertainty gave him back a small measure of his control. Without speaking, he covered her hand with his own and showed her how he liked the variation of long, thorough strokes interspersed with short, rapid ones on and just below the head.

Once she had mastered the rhythm and flicking, strong stroke that he preferred, he let go. He gently palmed her narrow shoulders and watched her face as she jacked him with a growing enthusiasm that gratified him deeply. His jaw clenched in pleasurable anguish. The water was a cool lubricant to her strong, pumping fist. She glanced up and caught his eye after a few minutes of agitating both the water and Tre wildly.

"I want to see you," she whispered fiercely.

He swallowed convulsively but acquiesced to her demand by slowly backing up on the beach. He stopped when the upper half of his cock poked up out of the water. Leigh immediately began her sure strokes, this time with increasing rapidity. Tre groaned at the way she stared fixedly at his cock in her pistoning hand.

"It feels too good, honey," he muttered eventually. "I'm going to come."

Leigh just nodded her head eagerly, her eyes never leaving his cock.

Tre grimaced as though he were in pain. Just before he crested he jerked up her T-shirt and pinched a plump pink nipple between his thumb and forefinger, watching as it darkened and pebbled.

He made a strangled, harsh sound in his throat as he came.

Leigh paused in her enthusiastic pumping when she saw the thick white liquid spurt forth from his cock. She would have continued to stare in aroused wonder if Tre hadn't put his hand back on top of hers and forced her to move up and down on him again.

She immediately conceded to his nonverbal request, stroking him through his climax, milking every last drop out of him. While he was still in the midst of orgasm she glanced up and studied his face. His eyes and jaws were both clenched tight with sublime release. That powerful image made Leigh want nothing more than to make Tre McNeal come again.

And soon.

The unwelcome thought struck her that if she'd never done this, if she'd ended up being only with Jim, she'd never have witnessed such a beautiful, sacred sight.

Her pumping fist slowed at the thought and then stopped.

Tre didn't seem to notice at first. He was still coming back to reality after his mind-splintering climax. But his eyes blinked open when he felt her unfurl her fist slowly and release him.

His neck bent as he watched her lower her hand into the water and make a swishing motion, rinsing his semen from her palm. One quick glance downward informed him that there was plenty more on his belly and floating at the top of the water. Christ, Leigh managed to always inspire a boatload of cum from him.

But this experience was new to her. She probably was embarrassed…or disgusted, he realized with a sinking feeling.

"It felt so good, honey. Thank you," he said.

She kept her dark head bent. When she didn't move except to shift her feet restlessly, he called her name.

Leigh finally looked up at him. The evening sun shone brightly behind her head, casting her upturned face in shadow.

"We should go, shouldn't we? Sarah will expect us for dinner soon," she said in a shaky voice. Without giving him a chance to respond she turned and made her way to the dock.

Chapter Eight
Present Day

When Leigh awoke later that night from a fevered sleep, her eyes opened into pitch-blackness.

"Tre?" she muttered hoarsely.

She'd been having a dream about that summer evening at the lake with Tre so long ago. It must have been the remnants of her fever that made the memory so heartbreakingly real. If she closed her eyelids she could still see the multi-colored hues of blue in Tre's eyes, feel the way the water lapped around them in a protective, sensual embrace as she kissed and touched him.

She felt like she'd been given a rare gift. The dream brought it all back with such vividness. The recollection of the fear and grief she'd felt when she heard about Kingmaker's death mixed strangely with her vivid dream of the lake, causing panic to sweep over her.

Leigh rose and fumbled furtively next to the dresser. She banged her knee clumsily against the brass bedstead as she staggered out of the room. Her voice sounded raspy and highly ineffective to her own ears.

Tre awoke with a start from the couch in his mother's living room. He glanced at the replay of a late night television show, wondering if the voices of the host and a famous actress and the laughter of the audience were what had awakened him.

He blinked heavily to clear his vision. It must be one or two in the morning. He'd only been sleeping for a little over an hour. He'd gone outside before midnight and cleared the driveway to make things a little easier for the farmhands in the morning. A half foot of snow already lay thick on the ground and it didn't look like it was going to stop anytime soon.

His mother had come home hours ago and watched anxiously as Tre gave a semiconscious Leigh another dose of Tylenol and ibuprofen. Although Leigh had still seemed warm to him he could tell that her temperature was nowhere near the raging fever that had battered at her hours ago. He'd let her continue to sleep without forcing her into the wakefulness required to hold the thermometer in her mouth.

He sprang off the couch when he heard Leigh whisper his name.

"What's wrong?" Tre asked harshly when he absorbed the sight of Leigh standing at the entrance of the living room. Her cheeks were damp with tears. She seemed dazed…desperate.

"You didn't leave?"

Tre hadn't stopped his forward motion toward her since he'd become aware of her presence. He pressed his hand to her forehead. His relieved sigh fanned her face. "God, you scared me. I thought you were going to be burning up again. You're still warm but…" He leaned back when his own words hit him.

"What is it, honey?"

She studied his features as if she were planning to sketch him from memory at a later date. When she spoke, her voice was the mixture of a sigh and a plea.

"Would you make love to me?"

For a few seconds they just stared at one another. Tre's eyebrows knitted together as though he was trying to solve a complex math problem. Other than that subtle movement his expression remained impassive. Only the flickering light and shadows caused by the television in the dark room animated his face.

"What did you say?" he finally muttered cautiously.

"I asked if you would make love to me."

His nostrils flared.

"This is the fever talking," he stated flatly.

She shook her head rapidly. A single tear slid down her flushed cheek. "Don't make me beg, Tre."

Tre despised himself for it but the ugly thought did occur to him that it would be damn satisfying to hear Leigh beg for him to fuck her. Not as gratifying as actually *doing* the deed but still...

He conceded that he must be no better than an animal. She'd just been extremely ill and her fever still lingered. She was vulnerable right now. But it didn't stop him. He reached down and lifted her into his arms. An uneven sigh rushed past Leigh's lips as he headed out of the living room. Their gazes clung as he maneuvered down the darkened hallway and into Leigh's room.

"There'll be no going back. You understand?" he said.

Leigh nodded. He kicked the door shut behind them and bent his knees to fasten the feeble lock on the knob. The room was shrouded in darkness. He paused with her in his arms.

"Is Sarah home?" Leigh whispered against his neck.

Her breath caused goose bumps to rise on his skin. The tremble in her voice made him grim. He lowered his head close to her face.

"Yes. What of it?" he challenged.

"I just asked, Tre. I'm not changing my mind."

He brought her over to the bed and set her down. He released her for long enough to flip on the bedside lamp to its dimmest setting. She looked sublimely beautiful to him as she stared up at him with her large, fever-glazed eyes. Her hair fell in a dark wreath around her face. Although her skin was paler than usual her lips and cheeks were appealingly pink.

When she reached up for him, Tre's eyes narrowed.

"Why are you looking at me like that?" Leigh whispered.

"You'll have to forgive me for being a little suspicious."

"Of me?"

"I'm expecting you to disappear any second now."

"I'm not going anywhere, Tre," she insisted hoarsely. Her forehead creased when she sensed his hesitation and saw the hard line of his mouth.

"Take off your clothes," he said abruptly. "I want to watch you."

Leigh felt her heartbeat pound wildly in her neck at his request. She sat up slowly and untied the drawstring on her sweatpants.

"Take off your shirt first," Tre ordered.

Leigh's hands shook a little as she drew the T-shirt over her head. She wasn't wearing anything underneath. Tiny needles of pleasurable pain pricked her nipples into full alertness when Tre inspected her through narrowed eyelids.

"Now the pants," he said tonelessly.

She lifted her hips and lowered the sweatpants down her thighs and over her knees. When she reached for her cotton panties Tre stilled her.

"Lie back," he whispered. He waited until she complied before he slowly drew the panties over her mound and down her legs.

A muffled moan exuded from her throat when he tossed her underwear aside. His glittering eyes never left the juncture of her thighs. Without saying a word his hands swept beneath her legs. He spread her almost matter-of-factly. But the expression on his face as he knelt between her knees was anything but common.

"Open wider." He waited tensely for her to comply before he leaned forward.

He brought his face less than a quarter of an inch from her pussy and inhaled slowly...deeply.

"Tre?" she murmured shakily.

But he looked utterly absorbed. He came down onto the bed on his knees. A sharp cry became trapped in her throat when he spread his large hands on both of her hips and began to tongue her cunt with hard, relentless strokes.

Leigh tried to shift her hips at the burst of explosive pleasure but he wouldn't allow her to move even a fraction of an inch. The feeling of his tongue as he slid it greedily along her sex lips then wedged it between the swollen folds to waggle against and vibrate her clit completely overwhelmed Leigh. One second her body had been humming with anticipation and arousal and the next every nerve in her sex was screaming a mandate for release.

He covered her with his hot mouth and suctioned her with exquisite precision while his tongue continued to lash at her tumescent clit mercilessly. His actions would have seemed cruel if they weren't creating the hottest, hungriest inferno inside of her that Leigh had ever known.

She vaguely became aware that sharp, surprised cries of pleasure were skipping unevenly out of her throat. She bit her lower lip hard so that the haze of mindless need receded slightly.

Jim used to love her with his mouth, it had been the way that he was most confident in pleasuring her. But just because another man had eaten her pussy before didn't mean that Leigh had ever experienced anything remotely similar to what Tre was doing to her. This sweet torture...this harsh initiation was something that would leave her forever altered, transformed by fire from the inside out.

"Tre...please...*please*...I can't..." Leigh whispered several moments later. Her neck rose weakly off the pillow. The power of relevant speech faded into oblivion beneath his sexual onslaught. She watched as his eyelids opened. His stare pierced into her even as his jaw worked her ruthlessly.

When Tre saw her mouth part beseechingly he tilted his head and aligned his lips with her clit. He sucked and ever-so gently bit the incendiary flesh. He watched Leigh's beautiful face constrict and her body shudder in climax and growled with deep gratification.

Making her beg hadn't been anywhere near as potent as granting her request.

Tre's eyes never wavered off her face and naked body as she rippled in orgasm. The sight pitched his arousal unbearably higher but it stunned him as well.

When she finally quieted, he allowed himself the luxury of dipping his tongue into her molten channel. Burying his taste organ inside her intoxicating essence felt like the height of decadence. He pushed his tongue further into her snug pussy, more than a little maddened. He fucked and vibrated her deeply until she moaned and tightened again with awakened desire. As if the shaky sound was his signal Tre came up on his knees and ripped at the button fly of his jeans.

"Move back on the bed, Leigh," he muttered thickly.

She followed his direction, utterly compelled by the sight of his tension-filled expression. His lower face was slick with her juices. She watched avidly as he shoved his jeans down around his thighs and hooked his thumbs into his briefs. He had to stretch the waistband far forward in order to free his straining cock from the confines.

Leigh's breath started to come in short pants of anticipation.

She hadn't forgotten how beautiful he was. The sight of Tre's cock wasn't something that any woman was likely to forget. But memory and reality were two drastically different things.

The only acknowledgement Tre made to her widening eyes and the nervous flick of her tongue as she stared at his cock was to take his heavy erection into his hand and lean down over her, positioning himself. He was too wild with his need for her to consider anything but the hot pleasure and immeasurable relief that finally lay in his reach after all these years.

He arrowed the head of his cock into her creaming entry and moved the shaft up and down slightly with his hand, prising just the tip into her. Christ she was small. He thrust but her deepest embrace eluded him.

His teeth ground together in frustration.

"Spread your legs wider and let me in, Leigh. I've waited too long for you. Don't make me wait longer." His hard, tense expression didn't alter as she tried to readjust her body to accommodate him. When she brought her knees back into her chest he grunted with grim satisfaction. He pried his cock into her clasping flesh another inch and transferred his hands to the antique bed's brass bedposts.

Leigh looked up at him as she gasped at air that seemed too thick for her lungs. Never mind that he was still wearing the gray T-shirt and that his jeans were rumpled down around his muscular thighs. He looked magnificent, like the primal image of a god poised to engage in an ancient sex rite. His eyes seemed to glow with desire when they speared into her. Leigh held herself steady when he thrust again.

Hard.

"Take it, Leigh," he muttered almost angrily.

It was driving him crazy to be denied her, even in this unintentional way. Sweat poured off his brow. He sank into her another inch, only to be halted once again. Her body held the first two inches of his cock in a mercilessly tight grip.

Leigh felt tears fill her eyes. He was pulled so tight with tension that it caused her pain to see it. She felt like she was disappointing him when he needed her so much. She lifted herself and pressed with considerable strength.

A tear leaked onto her cheek. The pain wasn't terrible. She'd felt worse. Her frustration at not being able to finally harbor him in her body was what really distressed her. She shifted beneath him and raised her thighs even higher, struggling to position her body to be more receptive to his presence.

Tre felt the give in her flesh. He gripped the headboard and pushed mightily. He groaned, barely stopping himself from shouting loud enough to wake not only Sarah but every living creature in a half mile distance from the farm. He was buried to the hilt in her. Even as his eyes opened wide in shock he began to pump his hips, withdrawing and spearing into her delicious heat again and again.

He was so maddened with his need that he couldn't stop himself.

"Why the *hell* didn't you tell me that you've never been with a man?"

He intimately knew the truth of what he'd just said. He'd never bedded a virgin before but recognizing one wasn't something you needed to have practice with.

Or at least not in Leigh's case it hadn't been.

It wasn't until later that he realized it had sounded like he was accusing her of a terrible crime, even as he proceeded to fuck her like the animal that he undoubtedly was. He tried to keep his thrusts shallow out of respect to her condition but it was nearly impossible. Maybe it was because of the fever but Tre had never been surrounded by so much heat. Her muscular walls seemed to suck him further and further into her depths until he was lost to all but the pounding waves of pleasure.

Leigh's eyelids fluttered open at his harsh words. She was still in shock at the sensation of being so utterly impaled and possessed by him. She felt so stretched by his conquering flesh, so overfilled, like he was pushing not just his cock into her pussy but his presence into every pore of her being. The feeling overwhelmed her.

"It doesn't matter, Tre," she managed in a shaky whisper as he plundered her with short, hard thrusts. "This is what I wanted."

She moaned. The burning sensation in the delicate tissues of her sex began to segue to a tingling, mounting friction that

Tre both built and alleviated with every lusty stroke. She instinctively began to move her hips in a counter-rhythm that left them both moaning and breathless. There was still discomfort but pleasure mounted exponentially with each passing second until pain was forgotten.

When Tre saw fresh color stain her cheeks and felt her begin to mutually mate with him, a fuse went off in his brain. He took her even harder, heedless of the increasingly loud and exuberant manner that the headboard of the bed and his own white-knuckled grip beat into the wall.

His path of vision narrowed until he could see Leigh and Leigh alone. He felt acutely aware of when her fevered lips opened into an O of disbelieving arousal and her eyes sprang wide. Tre released his hands, falling down over her.

He melded his mouth to hers as they both came and their shouts of muffled pleasure mingled and fused.

Tre pressed his forehead to hers a moment later as they both labored for breath. His heart pounded with alarming rapidity. He felt like he'd just been ripped open and turned inside out.

She'd still been a virgin.

Fuck. What the hell had he just done?

Neither of them spoke as their clamoring bodies slowed. But he remained locked inside of her. After another minute passed Tre realized with a gruff moan that he was fully erect again inside her clasping, hot channel.

Or quite possibly he'd never grown soft. With Leigh that was a definite possibility. How did one go about quenching a desire as thirsty, as immense as his was for her?

He lifted his head abruptly when she hoarsely said his name. The evidence of her illness gouged a guilt knife even deeper into his spirit.

"What?" he asked starkly when she spoke but he couldn't make her out because of her laryngitis.

Leigh craned her head up desperately.

"Mom. I think I heard her call out from the top of the stairs," Leigh managed tremulously.

That made Tre withdraw from her but barely. It was a wicked trial to endure. He hated to admit it to himself later but if it hadn't been for his mother he probably would have been fucking her again within the underside of a minute.

Leigh gasped at the sensation of him sliding out of her. She grimaced in sympathy when she heard the bitterness of his muttered curse. This time both of them heard Sarah's voice calling for Tre.

"Get dressed," Tre said tersely.

He helped her gather her shirt and sweatpants. Tre stood after a second and switched the bedside light to a brighter setting. Leigh saw that he'd already fastened his jeans and was running his fingers through his tousled hair. His motion stilled when he took in the sight of Leigh pulling her T-shirt over her flushed breasts. She saw his lips form one more curse before he opened up the bedroom door and called out in response to Sarah.

Leigh pulled the covers over her body as though trying to smother the fire of her desire, hide it from her mother-in-law at all costs. Her face flushed in dawning embarrassment.

She shut her eyes tightly in rising mortification. What would Sarah think of her? She'd been married to one of her sons and now was screwing the other one while she was a guest in Sarah's home. She'd be lucky if Sarah didn't kick her out in the snow right this moment.

How could she have abused her mother-in-law's trust in this way? Leigh had so convinced herself of a dozen dire ramifications for her impulsive actions that she froze in fear when Sarah entered her room with a concerned expression on her face. The older woman was tying a blue robe around her waist.

"I woke up thinking I'd heard a noise down here. Tre says that your fever is down but I had to come and check for myself."

Leigh couldn't think of anything logical to say as Sarah marched over and felt her forehead.

"Well, you sure are cooler than you were yesterday afternoon." Sarah turned toward the door and Leigh realized Tre had entered the room.

"I don't know though, Tre. Why's she so flushed?" Sarah asked her son worriedly.

Tre saw Leigh's lips part with panic at his mother's question. Why was she acting like she was so damn ashamed? he wondered with rising irritation. She was acting like she'd just been caught red-handed engaging in an unspeakable perversion. They were two healthy, available, consenting adults…not criminals, for Christ's sake.

He didn't immediately answer his mother's question as he moved with seeming casualness toward the bureau. Tre wanted to make sure that when his mother left he wasn't positioned in such a way that he'd have to exit before her. His eyes flickered over to Leigh where she huddled beneath the covers.

"She still has a fever but it's low-grade," he said.

Sarah's gaze looked uncertain as she examined Leigh. "Well, if you're sure, Tre."

Leigh realized that she hadn't spoken once since Sarah entered the room. "Of course he's sure, Sarah. He's been taking good care of me." She grimaced slightly and blushed when her words soaked into her awareness.

"My God, Leigh, listen to your voice. She's got laryngitis, Tre!"

Leigh couldn't help but laugh. "Well it's not Tre's fault, Mom." She glanced at Tre with rising amusement but her expression faltered when she took in his hard, impenetrable look.

Sarah smiled. "Well, I guess no mother is fair to her sons. I just can't picture Tre being handy around a sickbed. I know he's nursed enough animals to know what he's doing." Sarah's blue eyes skirted over to Leigh. "Not to make comparisons, sweetie. Now you get back to sleep, you hear?" Sarah leaned down and kissed her lightly on the cheek as Leigh whispered a good night.

"You're going to stay here as long as it takes to get you back to one hundred percent. I want your word, now, Leigh."

Leigh smiled. "Okay. You have my word."

"You coming, Tre?" Sarah asked.

"I'm right behind you, Mom."

A silence settled uncomfortably between them when they were alone again. Leigh studied Tre uncertainly but he was turned in profile from her. Anxiety weighted her chest when she saw how unreadable he was. When they both heard Sarah's footsteps at the top of the stairs and in the upstairs hallway, Tre finally spoke.

"Why are you so ashamed?"

Leigh was shocked, and more than a little hurt, by the cold anger in his voice. Was this the same man who had just set her on fire with his passion?

"I-I'm not ashamed, Tre. I mean, it was embarrassing, what if Sarah had come in while we were—"

"Fucking?"

A gasp left her lungs in a rush. His one-word question felt the same to Leigh as if he'd just reached over and slapped her. "What's wrong with you?"

"I don't like it when you lie, Leigh. You're feeling ashamed that you asked me to make love to you."

She shook her head helplessly. "I'm not, Tre. It's not that, I—"

Her words froze on her tongue when Tre stepped aside and lifted the photo that had been set face down on the bureau. He carefully placed it upright again.

It was her and Jim's wedding picture...the one that she'd been compelled to turn down before she begged Tre to make love to her.

She knew there was nothing she could say to explain her actions so she only watched mutely as he avoided her gaze and set some pills on her bedside table.

"Take those in fifteen minutes or so. They'll get you through until the morning." When he started to leave Leigh called out to him.

"Tre, it's not what you're thinking. I—"

His look of contempt before he stalked out of room effectively silenced her.

Chapter Nine

"Was that work?" Sarah asked when she saw Leigh hang up the phone. She took a bite out of one of the carrots she'd been peeling for the chicken noodle soup. Sarah'd grown weary of the leftovers from Jeff's funeral. She'd ignored her thrifty nature and dumped mountains of food down the garbage disposal earlier that day.

Sarah knew that it was irrational but she had the right to some unusual behaviors, didn't she? Her husband of thirty-six years had just died. Something about all of that food in her kitchen distressed her like little else had since Jeff's death. Conversely, enacting the familiar rituals of cooking soothed her spirit.

Sarah thought that Jeff would understand her actions, and that was enough for her.

She thanked God for Leigh. Having someone to make a good home-cooked meal for gave her the sense of normalcy that Sarah sorely needed.

And that girl needed a bit of pampering. She looked much better than she had yesterday but that wasn't saying much. Her face was pale still and Sarah thought she looked far too weak and skinny.

Leigh nodded as she set aside the phone.

"Yes. Ash didn't sound too thrilled about my not being there tomorrow," Leigh whispered hoarsely, referring to the head of the rehabilitation unit where she worked.

"Too bad for him," Sarah said with an indignant scowl. "Couldn't he hear you? You can't even talk, for goodness's sake. Surely he can't expect you to work with patients when you're so ill?"

Leigh gave a wheezy bark of laughter. "Haven't you heard? Doctors don't get sick. And if we ever do catch a little bug we know for a fact there's always someone else a lot worse off so we buck up and keep going."

"Hmmph." Sarah muttered eloquently. She pointed the carrot at Leigh. "It's that kind of silliness that undoubtedly got you so run down to begin with, young lady. When is the last time you had a vacation?"

Sarah shook her head knowingly when she saw Leigh start to defend herself only to stop abruptly. Her green eyes went unfocused, as though she were casting around for the answer to Sarah's question despite herself and had to travel back further and further in time.

"That's what I thought," Sarah said. "You've been running yourself ragged ever since Jim started getting sick years ago. Since way before that, I'll bet. You're an excellent doctor, Leigh. But your dedication shouldn't be getting in the way of you taking caring of yourself."

Leigh gave a weary grin and slumped down in one the kitchen chair. "I won't even argue with you, Mom. I'm too tired."

"My point exactly!" Sarah said triumphantly.

She turned and busied herself with her meal preparations. "I'm going to tell you what I want you to do. I want you to get back on the phone with that Ash person and tell him that you're taking some vacation time." When she glanced over shoulder and saw the protest forming on Leigh's lips she added, "Don't tell me you haven't accumulated a boatload of vacation time over the past several years."

"I have, Mom, but I have patients who need me."

Sarah threw out her trump card. "Well, I need you too, Leigh. What do you think of that?"

Leigh's mouth fell open in disbelief. Her eyes rounded. How could she be so selfish as to think otherwise? Sarah and Jeff had shared the kind of rare love that most people only dreamed about. Sarah must be dying inside right now, despite her outward show of staunch normalcy. "Mom, I'm so sorry. Of course, I'll call right now. I should have—"

Sarah set down the chopping knife, looking vaguely contrite. "No, *I'm* sorry, Leigh. I was being a little dramatic. But would it be so terrible, really? You need to rest and I...need someone to cook for," Sarah finished lamely with a wave at her preparations on the counter. When the two women's eyes met a small laugh burst out of Sarah's mouth.

Leigh smiled even though her eyes were just as moist as Sarah's.

"I'd love to stay and get fat on your cooking, Mom."

Sarah tried to hide the victory from her expression but she allowed her gratefulness to show. She brushed the tear from her cheek and picked up the knife matter-of-factly.

"Good! You could use some fattening up. I think I'll make some dumplings too. Tre likes those."

"Tre is coming for dinner?" Leigh asked disbelievingly.

She'd assumed he planned on avoiding her for the remainder of her visit. She'd seen Tre furious before but never so much so as last night.

Why did she always seem to bring out the worst in him when all she wanted was the exact opposite? In the cold, sobering light of morning Leigh knew that she couldn't entirely blame him for his volatility. Her behavior in the middle of the night had been erratic and strange. Leigh knew she couldn't place blame on the fever either, although that had undoubtedly played a part in it.

Sarah nodded casually. "He called earlier, wanted to know how you were doing. I told him that you sounded terrible but that the fever was almost completely gone. He waited until they'd plowed the roads this morning and went out to some stables over in Bloomington. He said something about a horse for sale on the Internet that he wanted to see but he was hoping to get back here in time for supper."

"Oh," was all Leigh could think of to say. She glanced down at her sweatpants and the pair of bright purple fuzzy slippers that Sarah had retrieved from her closet and forced Leigh to put on earlier. She touched her hair self-consciously. It was limp with the residue of sweat from her fever.

She cleared her throat to find the tiny remnant of her voice left to her.

"Maybe I should go and shower and then I'll come help you with dinner."

Sarah's sharp blue eyes reminded her of Tre's when she glanced back over her shoulder. "You go and take a nice, steamy bath. It'll be good for your throat and chest. Then you can take a nap or watch some television. But you're not doing any work, young lady. Not today."

Leigh repressed a smile, but her reply was docile enough. "Yes, Mom."

* * * * *

Sarah shivered when Tre entered at the side entrance to the house hours later. "Temperature really dropped since the snow, huh?" she called down the basement stairs by way of greeting. She hadn't been outside all day but she'd read the barometer and temperature gauge that Jeff always kept on the back porch. Despite the bright sunshine following the storm last night, the mercury was too far down in the bulb to give an accurate reading.

"Wind chill is twenty below," Tre answered matter-of-factly. He stomped the snow off his work boots and hung up his coat. When he glanced up the stairs and saw his mother's slightly raised eyebrows he bent and removed his boots. He lunged over the slush he'd drug in and climbed the stairs two at a time.

"Where's Leigh?" he asked as he followed his mother into the empty kitchen.

Sarah picked up a wooden spoon and stirred the pot of simmering soup. "She's taking a nap. I went and checked on her after she got out of the bath. She looked worn out."

Tre paused in the action of leaning over his mother's shoulder and inhaling the aroma of the soup appreciatively. "But she's not any worse, right?"

Sarah shook her head as she picked up a bowl of dumpling dough. "No, I think the worst of it has passed. Still, it was a nasty virus. Her chest and throat sound congested. She needs to rest or she'll be at risk for pneumonia, especially in this weather."

Sarah did a double take when she saw Tre's face stiffen with concern. She opened her mouth to confront him but something stilled her tongue. "She'll be fine, Tre. She's even agreed to stay for awhile and let me pamper her."

"She did?" he asked cautiously.

Sarah's heart squeezed in sympathy when she saw the brief, fragile flash of hope flicker into his blue eyes. She nodded and spooned the dumplings into the broth. "It's almost supper time. Why don't you go and wake her and see for yourself how your patient is doing?"

Chapter Ten

She was better, Tre acknowledged later that evening, but she wasn't fully recovered yet. After the delicious dinner, Leigh had insisted that she didn't want to return to bed, so Sarah had suggested that she go lie down on the living room couch. Tre had followed Leigh, hoping to have the opportunity for a private word with her. But Sarah followed soon on their heels with a pillow and blanket for Leigh.

"I feel like an invalid," Leigh murmured grumpily as she lay half-reclining on the couch, propped against the pillow and cocooned in the blanket.

"You sort of look like one too," Tre said as he glanced down at her with amusement.

Leigh stared up at him uncertainly. His manner with her had had her completely off balance ever since she'd gotten up from her nap earlier. It had been his deep, husky voice calling her name that had brought her to full awareness but the sensation that had stirred her from the embrace of sleep had been that of his firm lips rubbing sensually against her own.

Maybe she had been dreaming that part, or engaging in some serious wishful thinking. If it weren't for that evocative memory she would have assumed that his friendly manner with her during dinner was a show for Sarah's benefit.

But every time she'd dared to meet his gaze during supper she had to wonder. Leigh didn't know what had brought about the difference in him but he was obviously no longer angry with her. There was a warmth in his eyes that she hadn't seen in years. When Sarah bustled from the living room to clean up the after dinner dishes, Leigh stirred uneasily in the silence that followed.

"Your mother told me that you went and saw a horse today. What did you think?"

Tre touched her knees so that she drew them up, making room for him to sit at the far end of the couch. Her eyes widened when he casually took her feet into his lap and rubbed them through the soft blanket.

"I think it's a damn beautiful animal."

"Are you going to buy him?" Leigh asked breathlessly. She was acutely aware of her feet on his hard thighs and his massaging hand.

"Her. And I already did." He flashed a grin when he saw her look of surprise.

"Oh. You must have really fallen for her if you bought her that quickly."

Tre just nodded. "I knew her sire. It's not a purchase I'll regret."

Neither of them spoke for several seconds but Tre continued to rub her feet and ankles comfortingly. "Leigh?"

Leigh's gaze raced to meet his.

"Are you okay?"

Her eyes widened slightly at his quietly asked question. She knew instinctively that he wasn't referring to her illness.

"Yes...a little..."

"Sore?" he prompted.

She stared at her lap. "I'm fine."

He grimaced. "I'm sorry for being so rough with you. And for the way that I acted...at the end."

She looked up. "It was my fault, Tre. All of it."

His mouth hardened.

"If you think I'm apologizing because I regret finally being able to make love to you, you've got it all wrong, Leigh. Are *you* sorry for that?"

Leigh felt entrapped by eyes that dared her to speak anything but the truth. "No," she finally whispered.

Tre just nodded, an understated tribute to her honesty. He was about to test her courage even further. Tre knew that his own was being sorely tried.

"Leigh, when you get better will you...go out with me?"

"You mean like on a date?" she eventually asked in a wavering, scratchy voice.

"That would be the idea, yeah," Tre murmured. His eyes fastened on her with increasing focus. "But not just dating, Leigh. I want...I need to make love to you...more than just once. Much more."

Leigh inhaled unsteadily. "What about Sarah?" she finally managed.

"She's not invited," Tre said with a lightness he was far from feeling. He'd expected the question but expecting it and not dreading it were two separate things.

"Tre," Leigh admonished in a whisper. "I meant—"

"I know what you meant. I'll talk to her." When he saw the doubt in her features he continued. "She loves both of us. Even if she's a little put off, at first, I think you'd be surprised to find how practical and adaptive she can be."

His voice lowered persuasively. "Come on, Leigh. Don't you think you deserve to do something for yourself for once? Decide what you want but at least answer based on your own needs and wishes, not Sarah's or Jim's or your mother's."

Her lower lip trembled. "That's not fair, Tre."

He grunted. "As if anything ever has been when it came to us."

"We made our decisions," she said softly.

He just stared at her for a long moment. "Fine. You're right. I came to the same realization this morning. The past is the past and there's nothing we can do about it." Tre said with brisk edginess. "But what about now, Leigh? What about *right now*? Will you be with me or not?"

When he saw her hesitation he pushed shamelessly. "Just agree to go out with me a few times."

Her expression softened. She didn't even realize she was nodding her head until she saw the look of relief that lit his blue eyes.

A few times? That was what he wanted from her? Leigh knew that what she'd just agreed to would eventually cause her unbearable pain. She almost hadn't survived it ten years ago.

And she was more deeply in love with Tre as a grown woman than she ever had been as a girl.

Still, she couldn't resist him. After last night even the insubstantial hope that she could try had vanished like vapor once their passion had flamed hotter and brighter than ever before.

"All right. But…you'll speak to Sarah first? Or maybe I should…" Her nervous meanderings trailed off when he abruptly stood and leaned over the couch. His kiss on her mouth was hard and quick but potent.

Leigh expected she looked a little dazed when she glanced up at him when he stood. She hadn't seen him grin so lightheartedly since she was eighteen years old. Her heart squeezed in her chest.

"Stop worrying, Leigh. Have a little faith, okay?"

She just nodded once, too tongue-tied by the expression in his eyes. She watched helplessly as he left her to go help Sarah in the kitchen.

* * * * *

"Leigh? Is that you?"

Leigh's eyes widened in near panic at the harsh, all too familiar female voice. She placed the Tylenol carefully next to the box of condoms already at the bottom of her basket, hoping to obscure them from her mother's prying eyes.

"Mother, hello." She leaned forward and placed a filial kiss on Doris Peyton's cheek. A quick inspection informed Leigh that although her mother had said that she was too ill with her chronic emphysema to attend Jeff's funeral she appeared healthy enough...if downright irritated.

"What in the world are you still doing in town? I thought that you said you were leaving Sunday."

"I was planning on it but I got sick Saturday evening. I wasn't feeling well enough to leave the house yesterday," Leigh explained.

"Why didn't you call me? You could have stayed with me. But I guess you prefer to stay with your mother-in-law, is that it?" Doris asked aggressively.

"Mother," she murmured. She cast her gaze around warily, worried that other people in the drug store would overhear Doris' raised voice. "You don't understand. I'm saying that I couldn't even leave the house until just now."

"So you'll be leaving later this evening." Doris stated rather than asked.

Leigh hated the way she felt so cowed by her mother's bullying. God, how could her father have stood it all those years? How could she? She resolutely began to move past her and forced her mother to keep up with her if she wanted to continue the conversation.

"I'll be leaving sometime soon," Leigh replied evasively. "I see that you must be feeling better yourself."

Doris snorted. "If you call being in constant pain and discomfort better."

Leigh gritted her teeth in annoyance as her mother started in on a litany of psychosomatic complaints, only to be succeeded by bitter diatribe against all of her doctors and the medical field in general, for their ineffectiveness at helping her.

Leigh flushed in embarrassment when the young, pretty woman at the cosmetic counter gave her mother an incredulous look. She spoke quietly but with uncharacteristic firmness when it came to Doris, in order to try to counteract her mother's rising voice volume.

"Mother, I don't think I need to remind you that I'm one of those 'quacks' that you're talking about and you yourself are a member of the medical profession. It's hardly as black and white as you're making it out to be. You know as well as I do that the thing that would help your health the most isn't under your doctor's control but your own. You should stop smoking."

She flinched at the flash of hurt in Doris' lean face.

"What's gotten into you, young lady?"

Leigh just shook her head, inadvertently noticing the woman behind the counter's sympathetic expression. Given Leigh's history she couldn't prevent the surge of anger that she felt. She'd never been one to accept pity.

"It's nothing," Leigh said quietly. "Look, I have to get going. I'll call you tomorrow, okay?"

Doris' expression tightened with suspicion. "That wild brother of Jim's hasn't been hanging around you since you've been back, has he?"

Her sharp eyes must have noticed the way the color drained out of her daughter's face.

"His name is *Tre*, Mother. And there's no reason for calling him names," Leigh whispered. She was acutely conscious of the woman at the counter listening in on their inappropriate public conversation. "Goodbye. I'll talk to you tomorrow."

"There's reason enough to call him wild, and a few other choice things as well. I heard he goes for women who like it rough and tumble. You'd be way out of your league with that one. He's been with most of the single women in the county at one time or another, and undoubtedly a few of the married ones as well. Think I'm lying, do you?" Doris challenged in her hard voice when she saw Leigh's expression.

Leigh froze in rising humiliation when she saw her mother focus on the woman behind the counter who was pretending to straighten some perfume.

"Why don't you ask her? I saw *her* with him at the Fourth of July celebration in the park last year. She can probably open your eyes to a few things."

Leigh gasped in embarrassment. She could only meet the shocked woman's eyes briefly before she had to glance away in shame. "I'm sorry," she said before turning and fleeing.

Tears were still rushing down her face when she turned into Sarah's driveway and saw Tre's dark blue pickup truck. Yesterday before she went to bed, Tre had told her quietly that he would speak to Sarah today and that if Leigh had recovered sufficiently they would go out to dinner together tonight. The realization that Tre was likely breaking the news to Sarah about their plans at that very moment immobilized Leigh with anxiety.

Being rejected by both of her mothers felt like just a bit too much for Leigh to bear in one day.

She was still sitting there a few minutes later when Tre came out the side door. He moved with the long-legged, confident male grace that Leigh had come to love years ago. He'd put on a pair of dark sunglasses to ameliorate the impact of the brilliant winter sunlight reflecting off the snow. She noticed that he hadn't shaved this morning. The black whiskers that shadowed his jaw and highlighted his mouth made him look just a tad disreputable.

Her mind automatically flew back to her mother's rude allegations at the drugstore. She knew that Tre was the type of man who would always inspire speculation in others, especially women. Leigh swallowed heavily, beginning to realize for the first time the magnitude of becoming officially involved with him.

It felt a little intimidating.

She agreed with her mother on almost nothing. But still…wasn't there some truth to the idea that a wise woman steered clear of a man like Tre? Wasn't he the type of man who slipped elusively through your fingers just when you found out you were hopelessly addicted to him?

Leigh had lost him before in that way. She doubted she was strong enough to survive the experience again.

Nevertheless her eyes never left him as he made his way to her car, as though she were drawing strength from the mere image of him.

Tre's brow furrowed in puzzlement when he noticed how still Leigh sat. As he drew closer he saw her face. He changed direction mid-stride and headed toward the passenger side of her car instead of the driver's seat.

Leigh's didn't alter her downward gaze when Tre sat down next to her and slammed the car door shut.

"Hi," she mumbled after a moment.

"What happened to you?" he demanded without preamble.

Leigh couldn't help but give a small smile at his customary directness. She inhaled deeply, unconsciously soothed by the cool, brisk air that he'd brought in the car with him, accompanied by just a hint of his clean masculine scent.

"I saw Doris at the drugstore."

"Oh," Tre said as if her seven words explained everything.

He rubbed his hands over his knees briskly when he realized how much he wanted to reach over and touch her. He knew Leigh would incorrectly interpret such an action as pity. "That bad, huh?"

Leigh laughed mirthlessly. "I doubt I'll ever cross the threshold of Dean's Pharmacy again."

"Ah, well, that new one they put up across town alongside the grocery store is better anyway." The flicker of amusement that crossed her expression made Tre's anxiety lessen a little. At least she was looking at him now instead of keeping her chin in her chest.

"Tre? Were you talking to Sarah...about us?"

"Yes."

Curiosity mingled with the wariness in her eyes. "What did she say?"

"She said that she wants to speak with you about it personally."

When he saw her face tense he added quickly, "She's not upset about it, Leigh. It was just like I told you. She loves both of us. She's just...more worried about you then anything."

"Why would she be worried about me?"

Tre's mouth opened to answer but only a puff of air made its way out. He raked his fingers through his unruly hair. "Maybe you should let her tell you."

"All right. I will."

"But you're feeling well enough to go to dinner tonight?"

"Yes."

"And for afterward? I want to take you to my place."

Leigh swallowed convulsively, her hormones kicking up into high gear at the mere allusion to making love with Tre tonight.

Tre studied her closely. The unlikely but nevertheless potent thought of showing up at his mom's to pick her up tonight and discovering that Leigh had escaped back to Chicago kept occurring to him against his will. There was a world of uncertainty in her forest green eyes when they met his.

Still, her nod was resolute.

"Good," he said gruffly. "Because I've got a surprise for you, honey."

*****

At six forty-five that evening, Leigh sat on the edge of her bed. Her back was ramrod straight and her hands moved over her thighs nervously. She'd been ready for her date with Tre for the past ten minutes but she was too anxious to leave the bedroom and face Sarah. When she heard the light tap on the door, she bolted up off the bed.

"Come in," she called out with what she hoped was a semblance of a normal voice.

Sarah was wearing an apron over a pair of comfortable slacks and a pink sweater. "I'm slow cooking a pork roast so that we can have it for lunch tomorrow. How's that sound to you? Hopefully that'll get your appetite piqued." Sarah asked. She fully took in Leigh's appearance, including her pale, anxious face. "You look beautiful, Leigh."

Leigh brushed her hand nervously over the soft, light blue cashmere sweater she was wearing. She hadn't brought the clothing she would have preferred to wear on a date with Tre, so the black skirt and black leather boots that she'd had on when she drove down to Sarah's had to suffice.

"Thanks."

Sarah saw her hesitation. "I guess you're worried about what I think about you and Tre wanting to see each other."

Leigh just nodded but her anxiety shone through her eyes loud and clear.

Sarah sighed and sat down at the end of Leigh's bed. "Well, first of all, it's not as if I was shocked when Tre told me that you two were interested in each other."

"You weren't?"

Sarah smiled and shook her head. "No. Maybe it's just because Jeff and I know our sons so well. Or maybe we've just seen enough of animal nature to know when two creatures are attracted to each other," Sarah added with an amused glint in her eye.

Leigh licked her lips nervously. "How-how long have you known?"

Sarah shrugged. "Oh, way back when, I suppose. That summer before you and Jim went to college." She saw the way the corners of Leigh's lips went white with shock. "Leigh, come here. Sit down."

Leigh's face remained masklike as her mother-in-law took her hand and drew her down to sit next to her.

"Now, maybe I've never told you before, in so many words, how grateful Jeff and I were to have you in Jim's life. You were good for him, Leigh. I don't understand the reason that God took him from us at so young of an age but I suppose he had his reasons. But I'll always appreciate the fact that for the short time period he was here he was able to share his life with such a special young woman."

Leigh shook her head slightly but she found she couldn't speak. Emotion blocked her throat.

"Now, I know you well enough to guess that you probably are carrying around guilt for Jim's illness and his death. Maybe even enough guilt to make you not take a path of happiness when it's right in front of you because you think you aren't deserving of it."

"What?" Leigh asked, vaguely stunned. The conversation wasn't exactly going in the direction she had expected.

Sarah seemed preoccupied as she ran her fingers through her short, attractively styled gray hair. "Leigh, I know we've never talked much about your mother and father or what it meant to you to become one of us. But I knew, and Jeff did too, that when you took her wedding vows to Jim you were literally marrying into this family."

Leigh's hands covered her face in shame. She felt like Sarah had just casually spoken one of her most deeply hidden secrets. "I'm so sorry, Sarah. You're right. I wanted...I wanted to be yours and Jeff's daughter-in-law as much as I did Jim's wife. But that didn't mean that..."

Sarah made a soothing noise and brought Leigh's hands away from her anguished face. "Now, now. Don't cry, Leigh. You'll muss yourself for your date. Of course I know how much you loved Jim. Jeff and I never doubted it. I don't doubt it now. But he's gone now, Leigh. And you're still here, young and very much alive. And Tre is as well." Sarah shook her head and glanced away. "Leigh, I can only guess what you feel for Tre. But I know how he feels about you. It's broken my heart for years to see it."

"He-he left, Sarah. That summer ten years ago. He left and he never contacted me, never said a word." Leigh stopped as grief constricted her throat.

Sarah sighed. "Well, I don't pretend to know what he was thinking, what's motivated him through the years. I'm sure he's harbored his fair share of guilt about Jim as well." Her voice became more resolute.

"But I do know that he came to me today and told me that he meant to see you, honest and aboveboard. And I tell you something else. He brought up something that I wouldn't have considered unless he'd mentioned it. He said, 'Mom, Leigh's afraid of losing you more than anything'."

"He said that?" Leigh asked in disbelief.

Sarah nodded as she studied Leigh's face. "And I can see that he was right. Leigh, don't you know by now that I love you for who you are as a person, beyond your relationship with either one of my sons?"

"I had hoped it. But what if…Tre and I aren't able to…" Leigh floundered around as she tried to put her fears into words.

Sarah nodded briskly. "If things don't work out with you and Tre, how will things sit with you and me? Is that what you're getting at?"

Leigh made a sound of distress but nodded her head.

"I can't answer that exactly. I do know that you'll always be welcome in this home and at my table. I suppose a certain strain might potentially arise but I think we could get past it eventually. One thing is for certain. The fact that in your mind you were potentially sacrificing our relationship so that you could be with Tre tells me a lot about how much he means to you. As a mother that makes me happy for Tre. And as someone who loves you it makes me proud of you, Leigh."

"Why?"

"Because you're taking a risk. Stability has always meant so much to you. I know why and I can understand your motives. But sometimes you have to take a chance in life to get what you really want…what you really need."

Her eyes met Sarah's. "And you think what I want and need is Tre?"

Sarah's eyes twinkled and she pressed on her thighs to stand. "That's something only you can know, sweetie."

Leigh stood as well. She touched Sarah's shoulder lightly. "Thank you. As usual, your generosity has left me stunned. I thought—"

Sarah embraced her tightly. "I know what you must have been thinking, Leigh. I'm just glad Tre brought it up so that I could address it with you, hopefully set your mind at ease." Her blue eyes examined Leigh. "Did I?"

Leigh nodded. They hugged one more time before Sarah examined her. "You need to touch up your eyes. Don't worry. If your date arrives I'll keep him entertained while you finish getting ready."

Chapter Eleven

ಞ

"Tre, sit down. You're making me nervous."

Tre stopped his restless pacing and sat down in a kitchen chair. Sarah thought he looked extremely handsome in dress pants and a wool sport coat that seemed to make his shoulders appear even broader than usual.

She watched and hid a smile as he began to tap his foot rhythmically. She couldn't think of the last time she'd seen her son this worked up, if ever. If she recalled correctly he used to have short fits of nerves before his high school basketball games but they were nothing in comparison to this display.

All in all, Sarah thought it boded very well.

"Are you sure she's okay?" Tre asked for the third time.

"I told you, she's fine. We had a nice talk about you two seeing each other and we both might have gotten a little teary. Ruined her eye makeup, you know. She just had to...oh, here she is."

Tre stood up when he saw Leigh enter the kitchen. Their eyes met. Some of his anxiety faded when he saw her uncertain smile. She looked elegant and extremely sexy, wearing a skirt and tight leather boots that exhibited her shapely calves. Her sweater looked so soft and skimmed her full breasts so alluringly that Tre couldn't wait to touch her through it.

"I wish I had film in the camera. You two are the most handsome couple I've ever seen," Sarah insisted, partially to break the ice between two people that she cared about, and partially because what she said was the simple truth.

Tre grinned as he picked up Leigh's coat and held it up for her. "Stop, Mom. You're making me feel like I should have brought her a corsage or something."

Leigh laughed as Tre slid her coat over her shoulders.

"I forgive you for not having a corsage since you're not wearing a rented tux." She smiled when she turned around and met his gaze. Her bout of shyness burned away like the morning fog when the sun touched it. She lightly brushed her hand over the shoulder of the perfectly tailored jacket that he wore as if she were removing some invisible dust.

"You look very handsome."

His teeth flashed white in his dark face. "Clean up all right for a farmer, is that it? You look beautiful as well but it took you half the night to get that way." He laughed when Leigh opened her mouth to protest. He kissed Sarah quickly on the cheek and grabbed Leigh's hand.

"Come on, slowpoke, we're going to lose our reservation."

An hour and a half later Leigh watched Tre covertly as she sipped her wine. She liked to watch the hard line of his jaw as he chewed his food with slow appreciation, and the surprisingly sexual movement that his muscular throat made when he swallowed. Her eyes lingered at the V shape at the opening of his crisp white shirt.

Maybe it was the wine that made her say it, or perhaps it was the excellent food. Maybe it was the candlelight. Most likely it was just the novel experience of sitting and talking about anything that came to mind, with Tre McNeal—of all people.

"You were wearing a white shirt the first time that I ever saw you," Leigh murmured.

The fork that was filled with a succulent piece of rare beef paused on the way to Tre's mouth. He doubted she meant it to be but her voice had sounded low and seductive. It had the same effect on his body as if she'd just reached under the table and caressed his cock. He cleared his throat.

"You remember what I was wearing in the stable that day?"

Her smile was triumphant. "You remember where it was we first met?"

Tre smiled rakishly around the bite of meat that he forked into his mouth. After a moment of watching her with eyes made lambent by memories and candlelight, he answered.

"As if I'm likely to forget the time I walked in on you and caught you torturing my horse before you turned around and started doing the same to me."

Leigh laughed warmly. "Torturing, was I? I've never seen two living creatures like torture so much in my life."

He took his time in responding as he chewed, seeming to savor the taste of the food or the sight of her or both. When he finally did answer, it wasn't in the way Leigh had expected.

"You're really good with animals, Leigh. There are very few people who could have done what you did with Kingmaker in such a short period of time."

She was genuinely flattered. "Thank you. Believe it or not I actually thought about becoming a veterinarian when I was in college. It was because of my experience with King, mostly."

She sat back and smiled up at the young, dark-haired waiter when he refilled their wine glasses and asked if he could clear. For a few moments their conversation was held in abeyance as the remnants of their meal were whisked away and coffee and a dessert menu replaced them.

"Yum. Look at this dessert menu," Leigh murmured. "I wish I could have every one that includes chocolate."

Tre leaned back. "Maybe you should. You didn't eat that much for dinner. I hope you thought the food was okay."

"The bouillabaisse was amazing." When she saw his raised eyebrows she insisted, "It was, Tre. This is an excellent restaurant. My appetite just isn't back to normal since I've been sick. Mom's about to tear her hair out about it."

"You still are really pale," Tre said. "Maybe we should have postponed this for a couple of nights."

"No way," Leigh assured him warmly. When the waiter returned she ordered a slice of chocolate mousse cake to show Tre she was all right.

He passed on dessert but watched with narrowed eyelids as Leigh ate hers with almost voluptuous enjoyment. He was going to have to toss ice water on his crotch if she kept it up for much longer.

"I had no idea that you liked chocolate so much," he murmured huskily. Tre would have given the majority of his assets to have Leigh polishing his cock in the same way that she was sucking every last trace of chocolate off her fork. Leigh glanced over at him in surprise at the tone of his voice.

She licked her lips once, rapidly, when she encountered his obvious masculine appreciation.

"I guess that's the kind of thing that you find out when you go on a date with someone," she said with sudden primness as she wiped her mouth with a cloth napkin.

"Right. I found out that watching you eat chocolate makes me stiffer than wood," he said wryly before he took a sip of wine.

But this time Leigh felt less embarrassed by Tre's customary casual, graphic references to sex. "It was a good idea, Tre, for us to go out together like this. It's funny, how we've never had the opportunity to just talk and find out more about each other."

Tre nodded slowly. "Do you still like the work that you do, Leigh? On the rehab unit?"

Leigh glanced down as she stirred her coffee distractedly. "Yes. I love it. But as your mother has seen fit to remind me of lately, sometimes I think I get a little too involved in it. Maybe it's not...healthy."

"What do you mean?"

She shrugged uncomfortably. "I've been involved with the whole spinal cord injury culture since I was in college, mostly because of Jim." Leigh glanced at Tre, wondering how he would react to her bringing up Jim on their first evening out together but Tre just watched her steadily. "Jim was a peer mentor for guys with new injuries. I was really influenced by the people I met at the Spinal Cord Injury Association support groups that we would attend. Sometimes I felt like…"

"What?" he prompted when she fell silent.

Leigh picked up her coffee to take a sip then set her cup back down again abruptly. "Sometimes I felt like I was more invested in the spinal cord injury culture than Jim was," she said after a long pause.

Tre took a deep breath. "I know what it's like to feel helpless, Leigh. He was my brother and I loved him too. Your entire career has been based on you attempting to make the world a better place for people like Jim. There's no reason to feel bad because you've been so dedicated. I think you've made a monumental difference for every individual who has been fortunate enough to have you as a doctor."

Her eyes flew to his then quickly flickered away.

Maybe she'd had a positive influence on a multitude of strangers' lives but when it came to the life that she had most wanted to save she'd failed miserably. She stiffened when Tre reached across the table and took her hand in his own. When was she going to learn how to hide her thoughts when it came to him? He always had read her with alarming ease.

"Jim's death wasn't your fault, Leigh. At least not to any greater extent than it was Mom's fault or Dad's or mine," Tre said roughly.

"How could you even say that? How could you three have had an ounce of responsibility for his death?" Leigh returned heatedly.

"If it's true for you then it must be true for all of us. We should all share a portion of the guilt. All of us wonder what we could have done differently. But the fact of the matter is—and you know this is the truth, deep down—Jim made his choice in the end. I'm mad as hell at him for it. I hope that I would have made a different choice, if I were in the same circumstance. But who knows? Maybe I would have ended up throwing in the towel just like he did."

Leigh sat very still. "I was the one who was with him, day in and day out. *I* should have guessed how depressed he was becoming," she finally said softly.

Tre grunted. In truth he had never felt so angry with his little brother. How could he have acted so selfishly, knowing full well that Leigh would likely internalize the blame for his actions? What Jim had done was slower and more excruciatingly painful for everyone involved but he'd done the equivalent of putting the barrel of a gun down his throat and pulling the trigger.

"You were married to him. That didn't make you responsible for his happiness. Only Jim held that responsibility."

For a few seconds her eyes searched his. What she saw in Tre's depths made her tension lessen slightly. Still, she wiped furtively at a lone tear before she spoke. "The funny thing about it is that I thought he *was* happy. What does that say about my wifely powers of perception?"

"Leigh," Tre muttered tensely. It tore him up to see her like this. Still, this conversation was long overdue. It should have happened around the time of Jim's death, if not with Tre himself with *someone*. He could see that his brother's death had been slowly eating away at her.

"It says that you're human. It says that you saw what Jim wanted you to see, what he wanted all of us to see. Mom and Dad didn't even guess that he was sliding downhill emotionally and mentally until he started to show physical symptoms that were already dire. You know better than anyone that if Jim hadn't been paraplegic, if he had been someone with full functioning, the symptoms of depression and self-neglect wouldn't have had such mortal consequences."

"But you're right, Tre. *I* do know better what the consequences are...more than most people. And still I—"

"Couldn't have done a damn thing," he said with quiet finality.

Her gaze met his. Tre took heart in the fact that she was gripping his hand tightly now, unconsciously taking some of the strength and compassion that he offered her instead of blocking it like she usually did.

"There was nothing you could have done once Jim gave up, Leigh, especially since he wasn't asking for help. You couldn't have followed him around minute by minute of every day, ensuring yourself that he was doing his bowel program correctly or doing his pressure relief. He would have come to resent the hell out of you, and you him. He gave you no reason to assume that he wasn't doing the basic self-care that he'd done every day since he was sixteen years old. You're a fantastic doctor, Leigh, but you weren't *Jim's* doctor. You weren't his salvation and you sure as hell didn't control his destiny. At least have the decency to grant Jim his right to *that.*"

Leigh looked vaguely stunned by his impassioned speech. Tre glanced up in irritation when the waiter chose that moment to clear away Leigh's dessert plate. When Tre told him that they were ready for the bill, they were finally left alone again.

He stroked her forearm with his other hand until her eyes met his.

"I'm sorry about getting on a soapbox like that," he mumbled. "It's just that I can't stand to see you feeling guilty for it, honey. Don't you think you've punished yourself enough for something that you had no control over whatsoever?" Her eyes were wide with uncertainty. Tre could almost feel the way she wanted to believe him. Still, something was stopping her...

"What *is* it, Leigh?"

She looked away from him. Tre had to lean forward to catch her whisper.

"But what if...what if Jim somehow knew? About us?"

Tre's stroking hand froze on her arm. Christ, he hadn't expected this to be at the bottom of her guilt.

"You can't actually be worried about that, can you? Who knows better than me what a faithful wife you were to Jim?"

Her small smile was the saddest expression that Tre had ever seen.

"Was I, Tre?"

Tre wasn't sure how to respond to her anxiety that Jim had known about them. He'd never even considered the possibility. The thought of Leigh tearing herself up with guilt when she'd never been anything but a faithful wife made him feel heartsore.

He trolled through various memories from the past ten years, trying to re-examine his interactions with his little brother, looking for meanings that he might have previously overlooked—and which more than likely weren't there to begin with. But no, it was a useless exercise. His brother's warm friendliness had never faded, even when Tre had treated him with undeserved surliness on several occasions over the past ten years.

The most likely incident that *might* have hinted at the truth to Jim happened in the house that he lived in right now...in the bedroom that he tortured himself by sleeping in night after night.

Chapter Twelve
Ten years ago

ಐ

"You saddled up 'Boy too?" Leigh asked in surprise when she saw Tre leading both Kingmaker and Cowboy from the McNeal stable.

"Yeah, I thought we'd go for a ride," Tre answered. When Leigh automatically reached for 'Boy's reins Tre handed her Kingmaker's.

"I'm leaving tomorrow evening, Leigh. This will be our last lesson. If you don't ride King now you never will."

Leigh's eyes widened when they met his.

"Thank you. It's meant a lot to me. You spent so much time with King and I, and it was your vacation and all..."

Her voice trailed off weakly. She reached up and stroked Kingmaker's nose, trying to soothe herself. The reality of Tre's leaving suddenly struck at her like fingers on a piano, creating a poignant emotional cord of longing and distress...and loss.

"You know why I wanted to do it," Tre responded in a gruff, low voice. His eyes seemed to see far down into depths that she hadn't known she possessed. He held her gaze and a message seemed to pass between them.

"Are you ready?"

"Yes," Leigh whispered.

She didn't let herself think about what he was really asking her...to what she'd just consented.

They took one of the horse paths that wound through the farm for miles. Leigh felt so alive riding on Kingmaker's back with Tre never too far from her back or side. She leapt forward without a second of pause when Tre gave her a nod when she requested to give King free reign. Her body vibrated in shared exhilaration not only with the beautiful animal beneath her but also with the man who flew by her side.

Tre felt all of his concerns for Leigh riding on Kingmaker melt away when he saw her face lit with exaltation and her natural, graceful mastery over the powerful horse. He knew that his instincts had been right. Leigh may appear delicate but her spirit was every bit a match for the fierce animal that she rode.

They eventually slowed the horses to a walk as Leigh expounded on Kingmaker's perfections and Tre listened with gratified indulgence. He never touched her as they rode side by side. But as the silence between them grew, Tre became acutely aware of her subtlest movements, her proximity, the light sheen of perspiration that glazed her cheeks and chest.

"Doesn't this path lead to Grandpa's?" Leigh asked when she paused in her praises of Kingmaker and took stock of where they were.

His eyes narrowed slightly as he examined her. "Yep. Do you want to go inside?"

"Into the actual house? It's always locked."

"It's not like we'll be trespassing, Leigh. I have a key. They usually give one to the owner," Tre teased.

"Grandpa's place is yours?" Leigh asked in surprise. No one had ever mentioned that to her before.

Tre nodded. "Grandpa left it to me. Now I pay Dad to farm it for me. I think it's all part of their master plan to turn me into a farmer.

"You don't mind?" Leigh asked when she saw his grin. Her eyes stuck to him. She was always surprised anew by how magnetic he became when his face brightened with humor.

Tre considered her question. "Strangely enough, no. It's not going to stop me from doing whatever I want to do with my life. Besides, I like the idea of the land always being here for me." He shrugged, unsure of how to express his feelings in words.

"What will you do, Tre? When you leave the Navy in a few months?"

"I have some plans," he said quietly.

When Leigh encouraged him and drew him out, he eventually detailed his plans for his business. Leigh knew from Sarah that he had attended night school at San Diego State University over the past few years and had earned a Business Administration degree. What she hadn't learned was that as part of one of his projects, he'd formed an entire business plan based on a security software system that he'd written. Leigh always knew that Tre was smart but for the first time she felt the breadth and incising quality of his intelligence. It only multiplied his already considerable appeal for her.

Listening to him also made her feel not only their differences in age but also their more vast differences in experience. Self-consciousness slowly began to pervade her awareness as they drew nearer and nearer to Grandpa's—Tre's—house.

Tre dismounted in the wide, circular portion of the drive that led to the stable and barns. "You never answered me. Do you want to go in? I thought maybe I should look around the interior at least once while I'm here, make sure there are no leaks or broken windows or anything."

Leigh paused when he didn't wait for her answer but reached up and encircled her waist with his hands. She leaned into him trustingly. She was a little breathless when he lifted her down with so little apparent effort. The front of her body brushed over his belly and thighs lightly. Her nerve endings throbbed to life at the casual contact. He didn't immediately release her when her feet were firmly on the ground.

When she saw his expectant gaze on her, Leigh realized that he was waiting for her to answer his question. She bit at her lower lip nervously when she fully absorbed the intensity in Tre's electric blue eyes.

"Sure. I've always wanted to see the inside of this house," Leigh said eventually in what she hoped sounded like a casual reply.

"Here," Tre said gruffly as he opened her hand and put the house key in her palm. "Go on in and open as many windows as you can to air it out. I'll take care of the horses and come join you in a second."

Tre was right. The house was in dire need of an airing. Fortunately the heat wave that had caused them all to suffer for the past two days had passed and the temperature was currently in the comfortable low seventy degree range and cooling off even more as evening approached.

Leigh examined Tre and Jim's grandparents' home as she set about opening windows. The furniture in the rooms was old-fashioned and dusty. The house itself though was well-made with large, high-ceiling rooms and beautiful mahogany built-ins and wainscoting.

She was upstairs, opening windows in one of the second floor bedrooms, when she heard Tre call her name.

"Christ, it's hot downstairs but it's like a furnace up here," Tre complained when he traced the sound of Leigh's voice to one of the bedrooms.

"You don't have to tell me," Leigh admonished with a wave at her face and chest, both of which were wet with perspiration.

She stilled when she noticed the way Tre's eyes glowed in the dim room as they raked over her. Her nipples grew prickly at the touch of his gaze on them.

"You don't wear a bra much, do you?" he asked.

Leigh felt her cheeks flush with embarrassment in addition to heat. The room suddenly felt intimate and sultry when just a moment ago she had just thought it dusty and unbearably hot. "I...don't sometimes in the summer. I didn't think it was noticeable. It's a loose shirt," she added a little defensively.

Tre smiled slowly. "I wasn't complaining, Leigh. Your sweat is making it damp. It's clinging to you." His eyes rose to hers. "You have beautiful breasts."

The ensuing silence was as palpable as the rising tension between them. Leigh looked both wary and entranced as Tre stepped toward her. He didn't touch her but his body ghosted hers, less than an inch away. Leigh had to crane her head back to see his face. He dipped his head.

"You smell good," he growled softly.

"I'm all sweaty," she protested halfheartedly. She watched, mesmerized, as Tre shifted his head to the side of her neck and lowered next to her. Leigh felt like he pulsed against her life force, brushed sensually against some invisible energy field that surged with particles charged wild with electrical desire.

"I know." His breath caressed her hot neck. "I like the way it mixes with the way you smell underneath."

He glanced up sharply when he heard her soft whimper.

"You know that I'm going to make love to you now, don't you, Leigh?"

"Yes," she whispered.

He nodded slowly, gratified by her simple answer. He reached up and slowly begun to unbutton her shirt. When he'd finished he spread the material wide, exposing her for his inspection. His eyes were flames when they met her gaze.

"You're *mine*, Leigh."

The last tiny island of rationality that held out against the sea of desire that flooded her caused her to shake her head dazedly. "I can't be, Tre," she whispered softly.

A muscle flexed in his tense jaw. "It's not a matter of can or can't, honey. You *are*." His hands gripped her shoulders hard. "Tell me that you didn't feel it from the very beginning...tell me that you don't *know* it now and I'll never touch you again."

Leigh's face clenched with an emotion too powerful for her mind and body to hold.

His intensity shattered when he saw her expression. "Ah, Christ, honey, don't cry." His deep voice broke when he brought her against his body. "The last thing I want to do is make you sad."

Leigh shook her head as tears fell freely down her cheeks, wetting his shirt. "I'm not crying because I'm sad."

Tre tilted her back so that he could read her expression. "Why then, Leigh?"

"I just want you so much it hurts."

His muttered curse wasn't crude. It signified stunned gratification, his knowledge of the profound blessing of her honesty...of her existence.

Leigh encircled his neck trustingly with her arms when he lifted her precious weight into him. Neither of them spoke as Tre descended the stairs and carried Leigh to the first floor bedroom. The temperature was still warm in there but compared to upstairs it felt comfortably cool. The sheer curtain on the west window flew inward with a pleasant breeze.

Tre set her down gently by the bed. He swallowed back a wave of lust when her shirt fell open, partially exposing her high, firm breasts. She was flushed with heat. He hardened painfully at the sight of her thrusting breasts and plump, pink nipples, full and relaxed from the warmth. Leigh must have noticed his stare though because even as he watched her, crests tightened and darkened with desire.

Her beauty was something that stunned him again and again but he knew he'd never get used to her responsiveness to him. It drove him half wild with excitement every time he experienced it. He wasn't even aware of moving but suddenly he held her right breast in his palm. He feathered the nipple with his thumb. Leigh's ragged indrawn breath only heightened his mounting lust.

"Sweet woman," he whispered in praise as he studied how she peaked even higher under his touch. He leaned down and tongued the sensitive crest.

Leigh's knees almost buckled from the bolt of pleasure that flashed like lightning down to her clit. Her thighs tightened to try to alleviate the pressure that pulsed and mounted there.

His tongue felt warm and tenderly abrasive as he glided it over her sensitive flesh, seemingly intent both on memorizing every tiny, sensitive bump on her flesh and bringing them into further pronouncement. She gave a tiny gasp when he enclosed her with his lips and drew on her at first with exquisite gentleness and then with growing hunger. Her hand came up to cradle his head. Her back arched as she offered herself to him more fully. His hand found its way to her middle back where he held her against him firmly while he suckled. Leigh moaned desperately when he finally released her from his mouth with an erotic popping noise.

Her nipple was now dark red from the blood he'd drawn to the surface, pointed and tight. Tre grunted with satisfaction when he saw it and transferred his attention over to her other crest. By the time he was done Tre thought he'd never seen anything so erotic as the sight of Leigh's pale, thrusting breasts capped by two rosy, distended nipples.

Leigh knew that her own eyes must hold a reflection of the desire that burned bright in Tre's when he finally looked up at her.

"You're so beautiful, honey. Tell me this is what you want," he whispered gruffly.

Leigh nodded but Tre waited.

"It's what I want. More than anything, Tre," she murmured, knowing instinctively that he wanted her to commit to it with words.

Tre tore his eyes from the sight of her and scanned the bed. A cover protected the mattress from dirt and dust but Tre couldn't allow Leigh to lie on that. In the hallway closet, he found what he wanted. He paused when he returned to the room and saw that Leigh held the sides of her shirt together with a white-knuckled grip.

"Let go of your shirt. I don't want you to hide yourself from me ever again. It's too late for that, honey," he stated starkly.

He waited until her hands dropped and her high, shapely breasts were fully exposed again to his eyes. His voice sounded thick with lust when he next spoke. "Slip the shirt all the way off. I want to be able to see you while I make the bed."

She followed his instructions without hesitation, making his cock throb and swell in the confines of his briefs, eager to be set free. It was difficult to attend to the task of unzipping the plastic cover that held a soft, fluffy comforter and spreading it on the bed when his eyes kept returning to Leigh's breasts but he finally managed it.

"You're not going to change your mind on me, are you?" he asked teasingly when he was done, partly to cover his own anxiety that she might do just that.

Leigh's green eyes were wide when they met his.

"No, I just...haven't ever done this before, Tre."

Tre raised his hands to her narrow shoulders and caressed her silky skin with his thumbs. "I know, honey. And I want you to know that I'm honored that you've chosen to with me."

Leigh shivered at the impact of his touch. "I guess you have a lot...done this with other women," she muttered nervously at the same time the realization hit her.

Tre was older than she was and far more experienced. He was attractive, confident and extremely sexy. What would he think of her inexperience? She raised her eyes to his when she felt his fingers urge her chin upward.

"Not like this, Leigh. Do you understand?"

Tre watched as her lips parted in unintentional seductiveness in response to his words. She nodded once, her forest green eyes wide. She believed him, he could tell…and her trust was sweet.

He dipped his head. His kiss on her mouth was almost chaste in its tenderness. When desire overcame both of them and Tre's tongue probed the seam of her lips, Leigh realized fully for the first time that lust and caring weren't mutually exclusive. In fact, one only seemed to increase the strength of the other exponentially.

When Tre felt her yielding lips and heard her aroused cry, he bent over her and explored the intoxicating cove of her mouth. His tongue plunged into her again and again with a sexual cadence that made both of them groan with shared pleasure. He felt her eager hands on his shoulders and back. His kiss deepened as he told her with actions how much he liked her touch, how much he craved her taste.

Leigh reacted by aligning her body with his and pressing closer. Tre growled with approval at the feeling of her firm breasts crushing into his chest. He wanted to feel that sensation more fully, so much that he leaned back slightly and whipped his T-shirt over his head quick as a flash. Within two heartbeats his mouth was back on hers. He brought her even closer to him with his hands cradling a round ass cheek each.

When the reality of how perfectly they fit together, like two halves of a sexual template, Tre reached between their bodies and began to unbutton Leigh's jeans rapidly.

If it felt this exquisite to press into Leigh with all of their clothes on what sorts of unguessed-at pleasures lay hidden for him to discover in the depths of her sweet body?

Leigh's breath caught when she felt Tre unfasten her jeans. She stilled at the sensation of his fingers over her sex. Tre must have noticed because instead of immediately lowering her jeans, he slid four fingers into her panties and pressed up on her.

Leigh broke their kiss and said his name in an anguished cry.

"Shhh," he whispered. He watched her lovely face intently as he moved over her gratifyingly slippery folds.

"Leigh... do you know it's a dream come true for a man to find a woman this wet?" He smiled when she gave him a half incredulous, half embarrassed look and started to press her face into his chest.

"*No*, honey. Look at me. I don't like it when you run away from what's between us," he whispered hotly.

Leigh leaned her neck back so that she could see into his eyes. He smiled slowly at her acquiescence and dipped first his middle finger then his forefinger into her thickly creaming pussy, still holding her steady by squeezing her ass in one palm. He groaned at the sensation of her hot, clasping channel closing around him.

It was going to be a tight ride. The thought of causing her discomfort when she was giving herself so sweetly struck a discordant cord in him. Uneven bursts of air fell across his mouth as she panted while he finger-fucked her deeply.

"Just hold steady for a moment while I try to....ready you a little," he finished lamely. He watched her carefully, looking for signs of discomfort as he squeezed a third finger into her.

"Ah....God, that feels good," Leigh said brokenly on a sharp exhalation. She'd never been so full before and it felt wonderful.

Tre grunted in dazed agreement. He began to slide in and out of her. Her hips rocked against him with increasingly lustiness, making her breasts bounce enticingly. He couldn't unglue his eyes from the sight.

Christ, it was going to be heaven to be inside of her. He didn't think he could wait much longer.

He removed all of his fingers at once and began to apply a firm, relentless pressure on her clit with the flats of his first three fingers. She was so wet that he glided in her tender folds without the least friction. He saw from the way her eyes widened that Leigh was about to come.

"Suck on that," he ordered softly as his hand rose from her ass and palmed her head.

Leigh put her mouth over one of his dark brown nipples and did what he indicated eagerly. She licked him greedily, detailing every delicious little erect bump. When he began to pump his arm up and down, rubbing her clit ruthlessly, Leigh grazed her teeth across his sensitive flesh.

She fastened her mouth on him and cried out spasmodically against his chest as she came.

She came to full awareness a moment later, sitting on the side of the bed while Tre pulled off her boots and then her jeans and panties with rapid, sure movements. As if he was suddenly aware of her full conscious attention, his eyes flickered up to her face. He smiled.

"Maybe I should be gentler with you, Leigh. But I want you so much. And...part of this is...just me. You understand that, don't you?"

Leigh's hand came up to touch his lightly whiskered jaw at his uncommon display of vulnerability. "I know, Tre. I love your way. It makes me forget everything but you...but us."

His mouth fell open in an expression of surprise. She'd just communicated succinctly that she not only understood the fiery, demanding aspects of his sexuality but that his nature called out to something elemental in hers. It was what he suspected, what he'd hoped, but to hear her say it so generously almost felt like more than his spirit could bear at that moment.

"Lie back on the bed, honey," he said tensely as he flung off his boots and ripped at his button fly.

Leigh scooted back and watched, mesmerized, as he bent to remove his clothing. When he stood before her nude and unashamed as a young god, Leigh responded in the only way that could communicate her monumental desire for him. She opened her thighs and braced herself to receive the full impact of not only his large, teeming cock but the intense heat, power and vibrancy that was Tre and Tre alone.

Her arms shook as she raised them to take him in her embrace but they were strong and sure in their intent.

They must have been too preoccupied with each other to hear the sound of a vehicle on the gravel driveway but both of them startled at the noise of a car door slamming just feet away from the open windows of the front-facing bedroom.

Tre would never forget the image of how Leigh transformed in the matter of a second from being fully submissive and ready to embrace her desire to being strung tight with anxiety and fear.

In his dreams, her flat yet womanly soft belly captured the haunting moment. One second she had been welcoming, suppliant and eager to harbor his body in her own.

The next, her lightly muscled abdomen flexed hard with the guilt and remorse that Tre realized had always been always been regretfully close to the surface.

He moved back in disorientation when she rose with lightning speed off the bed and flew to the window, all the while careful to ensure that she didn't expose her naked body to whoever was outside.

That memory always stuck with Tre. He was so dazed, so caught up in the heat of the moment. He knew that he would never have even considered being so cautious, so prepared for disaster, like Leigh seemed to be.

He felt the first stirrings of a burning pain in his gut that would slowly eat away at him for the next decade.

"It's *Jim*," Leigh whispered. Her forest green eyes were wide with panic when she turned around.

Jim had managed to lower his wheelchair from his handicapped adapted van and to get himself into it without ever breaking her and Tre's awareness. Only when he slammed the door to the had their desire-induced consciousness been pierced.

Panic glazed Leigh's face. "What should we *do*?"

Rationality hit Tre, cold and cruel.

"This house doesn't have a ramp. If he wants to come in he'll have to bump up and he'll need us to help him with his chair," he said, reminding her of the technique that Jim had known for years of lifting himself out of his wheelchair with his considerable upper body strength and "bumping" up the stairs with relative ease, given the muscularity and dexterity of his upper body.

Tre hated the look of relief that shadowed her panicked features, even though he shared a degree of her emotion.

Leigh had dressed herself almost completely with the rapidity born of desperation when she finally noticed that Tre hadn't moved. For a second, her eyes lowered over him and she swallowed reflexively. His erection had lessened in the ensuing moments but his penis was still alarmingly full.

"Tre? *Please*...get dressed."

Her voice shook uncontrollably.

Tre's mouth twitched in frustration but he reached for his briefs and jeans. "Leigh, we have to tell him the truth."

"Oh my God, Tre, *no*."

His eyes widened when he fully realized just how brittle she was emotionally. Her gaze was unfocused as she listened to the sound of Jim laboriously coming up the front porch steps.

He gave a low growl of frustration when she hastily walked out of the room without a backward glance.

Even ten years later, Tre didn't know for sure what precisely had stilled his tongue after he had pulled on his clothing and walked through the dim hallway to the kitchen, where he heard voices. He'd had every intention of calmly and compassionately confronting Jim about how he felt about Leigh. He'd dreaded the encounter... hated the idea of hurting Jim. But he also refused to lie to his own brother.

Even more importantly, he refused to sneak around like he was a criminal for falling in love with Leigh.

Which is exactly what he'd done, he'd realized with a stab of shock and an ensuing numbness.

Maybe his fear first fully took hold when he walked into the kitchen and saw Leigh and his little brother sitting at the kitchen table, their heads close together as they spoke. Tre made the bitter observation that their hair was almost precisely the same color. It struck him for the first time that Jim and Leigh might pass as siblings.

More than likely though, it was the half-wild, pleading look in Leigh's eyes when she leaned back and met his gaze that had most effectively silenced him.

At the time, Tre had believed it was just a temporary postponement. But when Jim had died nine years later, Tre had still never had that crucial conversation with his brother.

And the anger that he felt toward Leigh for betraying what so clearly lay between them had only grown and festered from that day onward.

Chapter Thirteen

"When do I get my surprise?" Leigh asked in a mellow tone later that evening as she sat on the sofa in Tre's living room and watched him build a fire.

"You'll get it when I'm damn good and ready to give it to you."

Leigh made a miffed noise but in truth she was sublimely content. With the exception of her minor meltdown in regard to Jim at dinner earlier she thought her first date with Tre was going exceptionally well. She was a little anxious about going to bed with him again but most of those nerves could be put down to pure anticipation.

The temperature outside had stayed below zero today but Tre's house felt warm and cozy. She liked watching him as he built a fire. His movements were always so economical...so sure.

He'd taken off his jacket and rolled back his sleeves. Leigh would never guess that a pair of strong, veined forearms lightly dusted with dark hair could be considered so potently sexual but in Tre's case they were.

"Would you like some help?" Leigh asked eventually after she realized she was becoming a little hypnotized by watching him.

Tre glanced over his shoulder and their eyes held for a few seconds. Leigh couldn't have put into words how it felt to share such a look with him, to not see bitterness in the depths of his blue eyes. At one time, not too long ago, she would have sworn Tre would never again gaze at her with warmth, tenderness or amusement.

If it had been a gift back then, it was nothing short of a miracle now.

"The fire's built, Leigh." A smile tugged at the corners of his lips as he stood and sat next to her on the couch.

She grinned. "Good, because I wouldn't have been much help anyway."

"Not a lot of real fireplaces in those fancy condos up in Chicago, huh?" Tre said as he relaxed back into the couch. "Do you like your new place?"

Leigh tensed but only for a second, when he casually reached for her hand and held it in his own. "It's a little small but I love the location," Leigh said, referring to the condo she'd moved into after Jim died. "I can walk to the hospital every day when the weather is decent."

"Do you like living alone?"

Leigh stared fixedly at the leaping flames. "Sometimes. Most of the time it's pretty lonely."

Tre caressed her hand and didn't speak for several moments. He'd been burning with curiosity for two nights to know why she had still been a virgin after being married to Jim after all that time but he couldn't think of a way to broach the subject with her tastefully. True, Jim was a paraplegic but as Tre knew all too well he'd planned to have intercourse with Leigh when they were only eighteen years old. What had interfered with that plan?

"I was always surprised that you and Jim didn't have children," he said.

"We found out a few years after we were married that we couldn't," Leigh replied softly.

"Because of Jim's injury?"

Leigh nodded. "It's not the case with all spinal cord injuries. Many men can have children after they're injured but Jim wasn't one of them." She glanced up at Tre uncertainly. "He, um…could never ejaculate. But that wasn't the problem really, because they can obtain semen samples at specialty clinics. Jim had testing done though and his semen quality wasn't...viable."

Tre remained silent, all thoughts of wheedling the truth out of her about her virginity was temporarily forgotten in the face of her stark vulnerability.

He wanted to console her for something that she'd obviously grieved over but he couldn't say he was sorry. He would be lying. And he knew what a jerk that made him. But it had been torture enough to think of her in another man's arms for all of those years. To see her swollen with Jim's child probably would have outright killed him.

So he didn't speak, but instead sat up and took her into his arms. His embrace was the only consolation he could give her honestly so he gave it freely. They stayed entwined like that for several minutes, not speaking, each of them exquisitely attuned to the other.

"Are you ready for your surprise now?" Tre eventually asked gruffly.

Leigh sat back and swiped furtively at a tear that had fallen down her cheek. "Are you going to give me a hint about what it is?"

"No. But if you'd quit wasting time asking silly questions you'd find out what it is soon enough," Tre said as he stood and pulled her up next to him.

"All right, I'm ready."

True to his word, Tre refused to grant her an ounce of information but that didn't stop Leigh from guessing after they'd donned their coats and Tre led her to his stables.

"Oh, I know what it is. It's your new horse, I'll bet." Her eyes sparkled in excitement as they entered. Tre smiled at the evidence that the girl who had loved horses so much was still alive and well in her.

"Close your eyes, Leigh," Tre commanded. He chuckled at her automatic, enthusiastic compliance when she squeezed her eyes tightly shut. He led her over to the newly occupied stall.

"Okay. You can open them."

When her gaze focused, her expression melted from amusement to awe in a second. Her hand immediately went out to stroke the velvety soft nose of the horse in front of her.

"*Oh*...she's Kingmaker's, isn't she? *Tre*, she's beautiful."

He watched her closely, immensely gratified by her reaction, by the fact that she'd immediately recognized that Kingmaker was the mare's sire.

"You like her?" he asked huskily. The laughter that burbled past her lips was music to his ears.

"*Like* her? Oh my God, look at her! What's her name?"

"Ransom. King's Ransom."

Her wide, dark green eyes flashed over to him. "And I get to ride her while I'm here? Is that my surprise?"

Tre shook his head slowly. "Yes. But that's only part of the surprise. Ransom is yours, Leigh."

"What?" Leigh laughed.

"She's yours," Tre repeated. He avoided the dawning disbelief in her eyes, patting Ransom's neck briskly. "Of course, she'll board with me. I'll take good care of her. I doubt that they'd be too welcoming to Ransom up there on Chicago's Gold Coast."

Leigh's mouth closed then opened again. "You can't be serious," she finally murmured. Tre's gaze zinged over to meet hers.

"Of course I am."

Leigh's eyes reluctantly left his and returned to the gorgeous, sloe-eyed animal in front of her. Her hands went up to stroke the velvety nose that reminded her so poignantly of Kingmaker's.

"You are such a beauty, Ransom," she crooned in order to cover her inner emotional turmoil.

Tre smiled in appreciative amusement when she impulsively twirled around and hugged him.

"Thank you, Tre," she murmured into the side of his rib cage. "You knew how sad I was about Kingmaker...and about Jeff dying...and...*everything*. You did this to make me feel better."

"So it did?"

Leigh nodded her head avidly into the side of his body.

"Can we bring her out so that I see her better?" she asked after a moment of trying to bring herself under control.

Leigh spent the next half hour petting and praising Ransom. Once the horse was back in her stall Leigh glanced over at the tall man beside her. She knew that she shouldn't accept the horse. But she also knew that she would. It wasn't how much Tre had probably spent on Ransom that counted. He'd given her something more precious and elemental than just a lavish, expensive gift.

"What?" Tre asked when he saw her enigmatic stare. He stilled in sudden acute sexual awareness when he saw her slow smile.

"Tre McNeal, is this going to be a habit with you? Are you always going to use horses to seduce me?"

His expression unintentionally echoed hers. He raised his right eyebrow in amused arousal.

"Honey, if you require a new horse for every time I plan to make love to you in the future, there probably aren't enough of them on the planet. I'll have to figure out some other kind of animal that gets you all hot and bothered. What about rabbits? They're pretty plentiful."

Leigh laughed, amused and pleased at once. He planned to make love to her that many times, did he? That didn't sound like the short fling she'd suspected he might want to have in order to—what was that he'd said?— *purge* her from his blood?

As it always did, her heart seemed to bump against her chest erratically when she saw Tre's grin, the sight of white, even teeth in his dark face. Her lips still curved with mirth but her eyes became lambent with rising desire.

"It wasn't Kingmaker that got me 'hot and bothered' back then, Tre. It was you and you know it." *It's always been you,* she added silently to herself.

His smile faded. He reached out and palmed the side of her face in a fiercely possessive gesture. "Let's go inside, Leigh."

Leigh was ensnared by the heat of his gaze. She merely nodded, speechless, before he took her hand and led her out of the stables.

Leigh felt awkward after they'd entered the foyer and hung up their coats. She didn't have the mind-altering benefits of a fever to melt away her self-consciousness and restraint this time. Tre was in the process of removing his snowy shoes when she bent to unzip her boots.

"Leigh?"

Her hair fell back from her face when she glanced up sharply. "Yes?"

"Leave them on."

Heat rushed to her cheeks. She stood slowly and faced him in the shadowed foyer.

"Are you nervous?"

"A little," she admitted.

He reached up and tenderly removed a few strands of hair that had remained on her cheek. "I am a little too," he said, as though the realization had just struck him.

That got her attention. "You are?"

He shrugged. "You didn't give me the opportunity to get nervous about it the other night."

Leigh laughed softly. "Sort of steamrolled you, is that it?"

He grimaced. "Honey, we both know that I'm the one who..." He caught himself. He'd been about ready to say *power tooled you*, but that sounded too crude even to his ears, despite the fact that the description was a little too accurate for his comfort. "Was so heavy-handed," he finished lamely.

"It felt..." Leigh tried to think of a word to accurately describe his lovemaking. She noticed that he'd gone still as he waited for her to finish her sentence. "I didn't know that it could feel that good, Tre, that...intense. It was an eye-opening experience."

"I would have liked to have opened your eyes ten years ago," he said after a pause.

She glanced away uneasily. "That's not the way it worked out for us," she said, thinking how inane she'd sounded. Her feet moved restlessly. "Do you...want to go to the bedroom?"

Tre shook his head resolutely. He felt idiotic telling her that he was too superstitious to make love to her for the first time in the place where it had all started to go so wrong for them in the past.

"I built that nice fire. Don't want it to go to waste. Just give me a second." When he returned he carried the soft comforter and some pillows from his bed. Leigh was bombarded with memories as she watched him spread it before the fire. When Tre rose though, and studied her in the dim room lit only by the leaping fire, she didn't wait for him to make the request that she read in his eyes. She was getting used to his preferences by now.

Tre liked to see evidence that she was giving herself to him willingly and wholeheartedly.

She shrugged out of her sweater, dropped it on the couch and unzipped her skirt. He didn't move from where he stood several feet away from her as she stepped out of her black skirt and was left wearing only a black bra, panties, thigh highs and her boots but his eyes reflected the flickering flames of the fire.

When Tre realized that he was staring fixedly at her and that she seemed uncertain as to what she should do next, he finally spoke.

"Take off your bra, honey."

He throbbed with increasing urgency behind the fly of his pants when she did what he'd asked. The nylon bra she'd been wearing had been meant for aesthetics rather than support. Despite the fact that Leigh was no longer a girl, her firm, thrusting breasts still didn't require a bit of bolstering. Her skin looked flawless in the firelight. Her legs were just as finely shaped as he recalled. Her breasts had grown slightly fuller over the past decade but her hips and legs had retained the same lean, coltish quality that he loved.

He clenched his fists in restraint.

"Come here," he said.

The fire made the room comfortably warm so Leigh knew it had to be Tre's fiery eyes that made her nipples pucker tightly as she approached him. His gaze lowered slowly over her before his hands followed, gently grazing her collarbone, the sensitive skin at the sides of her breasts, the swell of her hips. She couldn't take her eyes off the hard, focused expression on his handsome face. When he urged her to turn around, she did so willingly.

Without preamble, Tre whisked her panties down below the curve of her ass. He stifled a moan at the erotic picture she made with her long legs clad in thigh highs and tight boots and her panties down below her beautiful bottom. He reached out and palmed her ass, aroused beyond measure by her firm curves.

"I told myself I'd go slow with you to try to make up for the other night, honey, but it's going to be more of a trial than I thought," he said wryly as he brought his other hand up and began to massage both buttocks at once.

Leigh glanced over her shoulder at him. Lust pinched at her clit when she saw the heat in his eyes as he watched himself massage her flesh. "Don't go slow on my account, Tre."

His gaze leapt to her face. When he saw the same desire in her large eyes that he'd heard in her voice he palmed the side of her neck and leaned down to kiss her.

Leigh's lust mounted higher at Tre's singular taste. She wished she could submerse herself in it. Despite the fact that she loved the way he was palming her ass with such unapologetic relish she turned decisively in his arms and began unbuttoning his shirt even as she craned her head back and participated eagerly in his hot kiss. She'd fantasized too many times about what it would be like to have Tre's beautiful body stretched out before her like an adult playground for her hedonistic enjoyment to pass up the opportunity while it stood right next to her.

Tre couldn't help but smile in amusement when Leigh proceeded to undress him as if she believed she was participating in a timed contest. "Take it easy, honey. I'm not going anywhere. Neither is that," he murmured more thickly when she lowered his briefs over his cock and it sprang forth eagerly into her awaiting hand.

Leigh caressed him from base to tip experimentally. He felt like power personified in her stroking palm.

Tre allowed her to run her hand up and down him a few more times while he watched steadily but when her magical fingertips curiously explored his testicles he stopped her.

"Let's lie down or this is going to be over before we ever got started," Tre said. He hooked her panties with his thumbs and whisked them down her thighs and over her boots until she stepped out of them while she steadied herself with her hands on his shoulders.

Leigh looked a little disappointed but dazedly knelt on the comforter when Tre glanced down significantly. "I want to be able to touch you everywhere," she said in a low, passionate voice when Tre had removed his pants and socks and came down beside her on the comforter, naked. Her gaze toured the veritable mountain of hard, lean male flesh next to her.

Tre's eyebrows rose with prurient interest at the uninhibited hunger in her large eyes. The evidence of her enthusiasm when it came to sex was a pleasant—and arousing—surprise.

"Far be it from me to discourage you."

Leigh licked her lower lip as anxiety and desire warred inside of her. "I'm not sure that I...know exactly what you'll like. I haven't done this much, Tre."

It was on the tip of his tongue to demand her to tell him why she didn't have much experience with making love to a man when she said starkly, "Jim was...self-conscious about his body...more so in the later years than in the beginning."

A frisson of uncertainty went through Leigh when she saw his unreadable expression. Why did she keep bringing up Jim when she was on a date with Tre—when she was in the midst of making love with him, for God's sake? What a turn off that must be.

Tre swallowed back his pointed follow-up question. Now wasn't the time to satisfy his masochistic curiosity when it came to her relationship with his brother.

"Just touch me, Leigh, any way you like. I'll let you know what I want when the thought occurs to me," he assured her before he palmed the back of her neck and gave her a kiss that he hoped adequately communicated to her that she could merely blink and breathe and he'd be aroused.

He allowed her to break their increasingly carnal, sensual kiss after several moments, groaning in appreciation when she turned the attention of her soft lips and quick tongue to his ear and then his neck. He tensed when she found the sensitive spot at his nape. Arousal prickled his skin. As if she sensed this perfectly, her fingers locked in on his nipple the second after it'd pulled tight.

"Leigh," he muttered in a gravelly voice. *And she'd suggested that she didn't know what he would like*, he thought wryly. He noticed her bewitching, small smile before she ducked her head and began nipping at his chest, seemingly testing out his textures against her sensitive lips while her forefinger continued to rub and create friction against his stiffening nipple. Without conscious thought his hand rose to her head and he guided her mouth to the flesh she was teasing to such pleasurable effect.

"Suck, honey," he whispered hoarsely.

Leigh immediately created a vacuum over the sensitive, flat disc. Her hand, meanwhile, explored his rib cage and abdomen, liking the way her touch made his muscles flex and his skin roughen.

Tre leaned back on his hands while Leigh tortured him with her light, skimming fingertips and warm mouth, which continued to tug at and taunt his nipple. He had to do something with his hands because the primitive urge to lay her on her back, sink into her and fuck her until all rational thought dissolved from his brain nearly overwhelmed him. He clenched his jaw as he watched her fasten her mouth on his other nipple and take his penis into her hand.

Leigh moaned against his chest at the feeling of his cock. The warm column of thick flesh felt smooth and taut against her hand, like the skin had been stretched tighter than a drum from his teeming desire. She released his nipple from her mouth and dropped her forehead to inspect what she held. She wasn't offended when Tre lifted his hand from the comforter and wordlessly pressed her head down to him because their desires were in perfect synchrony at that moment.

He watched through narrowed eyelids as she held his cock steady at the base and her red tongue touched the tip experimentally. He inhaled slowly to calm his raging lust when her initial uncertainty faded and she began to polish the entire head in earnest. Tre could tell that she'd never done this before but her eager generosity touched him as much as it piqued his lust.

Hoping that he wasn't dulling the edge of her gratifying enthusiasm, he gruffly told her what he wanted. His eyes rolled back in his head and sweat popped out on his brow when she stretched her jaw and took him between her pursed lips. He felt like every muscle in his body pulled tight when she fluttered her tongue over him at first curiously and then with increasing ardency.

"Suck, honey. Just like you did on my nipple," he directed.

He groaned gutturally when she tightened her lips around him and did just that.

She might not have the experience but she was born with the talent. He indicated what he desired, this time by gently applying pressure at the back of her head instead of with words. He forced himself to look up into the fire when she began to slide him in and out of her tightly clasped lips. The sight of her jaw and lips stretched so wide to accommodate him was the image of the paradox of blissful agony.

"Careful," he whispered after a several tense moments when she drew him deeper into her suctioning heat. When she ignored him, however, and he sensed her determination, he urged her up off of him despite his more primitive desires.

Even if it was just a fantasy, he hoped to be making love with Leigh for as long as she'd let him. The last thing he wanted to do was to ruin the experience for her by getting so lost in the experience that he caused her to gag. He had occasion to despise some faceless, nameless jerks that had spoilt oral sex for a few women that he'd been with in the past in that way.

Damn if he was going to do that to Leigh.

Leigh murmured incoherently in protest when she felt Tre's hands on her shoulders, lifting her. When she glanced up at him she saw how rigid the lean muscles all over his body were pulled. Her thwarted desire was forgotten when he scooted back against the couch and encouraged her to spread her thighs.

"Take me, honey," he said tensely as he poised his cock in his hand and guided her hip with the other. When her awkwardness finally penetrated his thick arousal, he added, "Put your hands up on my shoulders. That's right. Come down slowly."

Leigh gasped at the sensation of his broad head arrowing into her pussy and filling her inch by inch. Her eyes flickered up to meet his gaze.

"Pain?" Tre asked tautly.

"No," she whispered. "It feels so good." She reinforced her point by sinking him deeper into her flesh. Tre grunted in tense appreciation. Like the first time, he stretched her delicate tissues seemingly to the limit but there was no pain. She eased down until his entire length was embedded and the lower curve of her ass rested on his thighs. His girth was so wide that she felt a hot friction slowly start to build not only in her pussy, but where he inadvertently applied pressure on her clitoris...and even her anus.

Tre studied Leigh's sweat-glistening face, fascinated by her expression of stunned arousal. He palmed one round buttock, readying her for his thrusts before he leaned forward and took the crest of one pointed breast into his mouth. When he felt Leigh's muscular, snug channel tighten around him he began to urge her up and down on his length. He pulled on her nipple more urgently at the immensity of the pleasure before releasing it and fastening his mouth on the other tight, rosy crest, mindlessly ecstatic at the feast before him.

After a moment Leigh began to use his shoulders and her flexing thighs in order to ride his cock, adding her own strength and weight to Tre's already demanding thrusts. Her eyes went wide at the sharp, singeing quality of the pleasure. She cried out brokenly when Tre spread both of his big hands over her hips and ass and began plunging her down over his cock with breathtaking power, setting a ruthless pace. Their flesh made contact with quick, succinct smacking noises, her disbelieving cries of pleasure mixed together with his gratified grunts against her breast.

He released her nipple and leaned back on the couch, watching his cock slide in and out of her. He had to use all of his willpower not to come inside of her with each inward stroke. She was milking him like a warm, velvet-lined fist. Now that he'd released her breast from his mouth he could see that their increasingly enthusiastic lovemaking made her luscious breasts bob up and down each time their bodies crashed together. The image made him tighten his grip on her hips and still her for a moment.

He clenched his eyes shut, trying to gain a small measure of control.

Leigh gave a cry of disappointment when Tre held firmly down in his lap, preventing her from moving. Her eyes fluttered open and focused. Desire hazed her vision. He looked magnificent. His chest and arm muscles were flexed with tension. A light sheen of sweat glistened on his torso. His small, dark brown nipples were stiff and distended.

Tre heard Leigh's soft cry and felt her shift her hips forward. Knowing where she was seeking friction he reached for her, offering it with his massaging thumb. It must have been divine intervention that allowed him to survive the sensual torture of feeling her pussy spasm around and pull at his cock while her beautiful face collapsed with pleasure. He groaned when she gyrated her hips in small, tight circles around his cock to feed and amplify her climax.

By the time she'd quieted and started to sag against him, Tre lifted her with a grim, determined expression on his face. Leigh whimpered when he withdrew and placed her on her knees next to him.

"Turn around and put your elbows on the couch," he told her shortly. Almost all his available energy was going into staving off a scalding orgasm for just a minute longer. His cock felt ponderous and heavy when he took it into his palm. He couldn't stop himself from pumping while Leigh positioned herself on her knees leaning over the seat of the couch. She looked like one of his many graphic fantasies concerning her come to life, but even more beautiful than he'd ever imagined.

He trailed one hand against her nylons and the silky skin of her thigh before he grabbed one ass cheek. He pushed back on her, exposing her glossy, swollen cunt to his hungry gaze, both parting her and positioning her.

He plunged into her with one long, hard stroke. A guttural curse tore from his throat.

Leigh's mouth sagged open at the impact of him slicing so deeply into her being and then setting a punishing pace. She used her elbows to brace herself as best as she could as he crashed into her pussy again and again, or else she would have spilled forward at the forceful impact. She'd never felt so filled, so overwhelmed, like he was relentlessly battering away at and smashing to pieces every last defense she might have carefully erected against him. The realization made her cry out in uncertainty. She fell forward with a whimper.

But Tre would have none of it. He gripped her hips and pulled her back to her original position.

"I'm not hurting you, am I?" Tre rasped.

Leigh looked over her shoulder and shook her head rapidly. It hadn't been pain that had made her pull away from him.

"Does it feel good?"

"God, yes," she whispered.

"Then hold still," he ordered, even as his hips and buttocks began their powerful thrusting once again. Just in case she planned on resisting him again, he fixed her in place with a resolute hold on her hips.

Leigh did what he demanded, keeping herself as still as possible. She bit her lip as the unbearable tension mounted with each pass of his conquering cock. The pressure splintered gloriously the third time when he crashed his pelvis against her and jerked up slightly on her bottom with his muscular arms, applying pressure to her clit like a smart bomb. She sobbed as orgasm shattered not only her flesh but her spirit. She was vaguely aware of Tre jerking his cock out of her, his roar of completion as he held her hip steady…the feeling of his warm cum spurting on her ass.

Tre's breath soughed raggedly into her left ear where he was leaning over her. She became aware of the cooling wetness on her backside. Her orgasm had been so explosive it must have rattled her brain loose from her skull. She groaned miserably.

"What's wrong?" Tre asked in a gravelly voice next to her ear.

Leigh turned her flushed cheek into the couch and looked into his eyes. "I brought condoms to use. I should have gotten one out before we ever got started."

Tre didn't respond immediately. Instead he flexed his arms and stood up behind her. When he saw her start to turn around he told her to sit still for a second. When he returned, he carried a damp washcloth and a towel. Leigh twisted around so that she could see his face as he knelt behind her and tenderly used the warm cloth to remove all the cum from her bottom. Afterward he bent and unzipped her boots and removed them.

"Come here, honey," he murmured once he'd dried her off with the towel. Leigh lowered her body next to him on the comforter and went into his arms. He kissed her ear. "It was my fault. I have condoms too. I just get carried away when I'm with you. I won't let it happen again. Okay?"

Leigh just nodded into his chest. For a minute neither of them spoke, appreciating the feeling of being in each other's arms and the flickering firelight. But eventually Tre's satiation ebbed and his damnable curiosity got the better of him.

"Leigh? Why were you still a virgin?"

Chapter Fourteen

ଛ

"Surely it's not that big of a shock to you, Tre," she murmured evasively. "Jim couldn't make love in that way."

"Yes he could, Leigh." He noticed when she glanced up at him warily. "I went with him on the day that he decided to ask Dr. Conway for one of those drugs that would give him an erection. Are you saying that it didn't work for him?"

A shiver coursed over Leigh's naked skin. Her brief laugh was mirthless. It made her feel more vulnerable than she could put into words to know that Tre had known about Jim's plans all those years ago.

"Those drugs are pretty foolproof, Tre. You take it…bingo. You get hard. For some couples they're indispensable."

"But they weren't for you and Jim?" Tre tensed in protest when she struggled against him and rose to a sitting position. For a few seconds he was faced with the daunting prospect of her bared back.

"Do we have to talk about this right now?" Leigh eventually asked.

His jaw clamped tightly when he saw the expression on her face.

"No. I know I don't have a right to ask."

Leigh lowered herself on top of him. She stifled a groan at the exquisite sensation of his hair-roughened skin abrading her softness. "You do have a right to know, Tre. I just don't want to talk about it now. I just want to enjoy this." She glanced downward to where their bodies pressed tightly together. Her breasts were pale next to his dark chest hair and skin. Both of them appreciated the sight for a moment before Tre took her in both of his hands and fondled her.

"Is this what you want?"

Her eyes darkened with passion despite the roughness of his question.

"Yes, Tre," she whispered, giving him only the smooth surface of her love instead of the ragged edges of her irritation onto which he could fasten his own anger.

He gave a small smile, knowing he'd been soothed, if a little unsure as to how.

"If that's what you want, lean down and give me these," he said gruffly as he whisked his thumbs across her erect nipples. "God knows I've got plenty of that to give you."

* * * * *

"Tre, wake up. It'll be dawn in awhile. You have to take me back to Sarah's."

Tre reached out blindly from the deep embrace of sleep and palmed a smooth hip. He groaned with satisfaction and shifted his hand to a firm ass cheek. He squeezed.

"Tre," Leigh admonished. "I didn't wake you up for that. Surely it's not possible for us to do it again after all those times before—"

Her eyes widened and a puff of air flew past her lips. He'd begun to jiggle her bottom in a manner that was downright lewd. The dying fire cast the room in shadows but still Leigh saw when Tre sat up from his reclining position and leaned over her as she lay on her belly, watching what his hands did to her flesh in the dim light.

"Have I ever told you what a lech I have for your ass, Leigh?" he asked in a sleep-roughed voice.

Leigh swallowed convulsively. "Uh...no."

He continued to jiggle upward on her ass from where he palmed her bottom, enjoying the sight of her bobbing, plump cheeks immensely.

"It's not time to go yet, Leigh," he whispered roughly next to her bottom before he kissed her once hotly on her right cheek.

"Oh but—"

"Leigh," he said warningly before he sent one long finger between her legs and into her damp, warm pussy. She squirmed. He bit gently at her wriggling ass and used his other hand to spread her cheeks.

"It's not time yet."

Leigh groaned and clenched her eyes shut. Christ it felt good.

"No, not time yet," she mumbled in breathless agreement.

"What are you so grouchy about?" Leigh wondered when Tre closed the door to his truck so hard it rocked the cab. She shared in his irritability. It had been pure torture to part from his warm embrace. When she stepped outside, the subzero, pre-dawn temperature made her want to cry like a baby that had just left its mother's protective womb.

Tre glanced over at her with asperity. "This is ridiculous and you know it. My mother knows that you're perfectly safe over here with me. She also knows what we've been doing all damn night."

He started the truck with a flick of his wrist. Leigh gritted her teeth with frustration as she watched him back rapidly out of the long driveway with the casual expertise born of being raised a farmboy. Neither of them spoke for the few minutes that it took him to get to his mother's house.

"I want to you get your things and come and stay with me," he said once he'd parked the car in Sarah's driveway.

"That's outrageous."

"No, I'll tell you what's outrageous, Leigh," he barked. "It's ridiculous that we've finally come together after all this time and I don't even get the pleasure of waking up next to you. How long are you going to make us sneak around like we're a couple of criminals or something? The first time it was Jim you had to protect. Now you have to shield Mom from the terrible truth about us. When the fuck are you going to come to me freely, Leigh?"

Leigh gaped at him.

"Maybe when you stop being angry at me for God knows what," she hissed furiously.

Hurt crowded into her awareness that he would spin the truth so crazily because of some grudge he held against her for marrying Jim. It pained her like little else could have. "How could you speak to me like that after tonight?"

When his only reaction was to turn his head and stare out the front window she continued, "Your mother asked me specifically to stay with her. I think it's helped to have someone here who she can cook for and pamper."

"Thanks for emphasizing the fact that I'm a selfish, asshole son to boot," he said woodenly.

But this time Leigh wasn't having any of it. "Why shouldn't I? You seem to have no problem making me sound like I'm a frigid bitch. Don't you know how much I want to be back sleeping in your arms right now? It killed me to pry myself away from you. It still is. And then you have to go and make it worse by making me into some sadistic, unfeeling—"

She paused when Tre ducked his head abruptly and pulled her into his arms.

"I'm sorry," he murmured into her neck. "You make me a little crazy, Leigh. Of course you're right. Mom needs you right now."

Leigh breathed out in exasperation. She turned her head, catching his rich, masculine scent. Her irritation seeped out of her. Part of her knew that Tre's anger toward her needed to be resolved...but not now. Not after they'd spent such a carnal, spiritually rending night together.

Her eyes burned from exhaustion and emotional unrest. She kissed his whisker-roughed cheek softly.

"I should go."

He nodded and released her from his arms.

"Leigh?" Tre said harshly when she opened the door of his truck. He waited until she'd turned to face him. "I'll see you tomorrow?"

Leigh smiled slowly. "You'll see me later today, Tre."

* * * * *

Tre hit the brakes on his car when he flew past the drive to his own house on the way to his mother's later that afternoon. He and his lawyer had just met in Champaign with a representative from a huge conglomerate. He'd decided to devote a larger portion of acreage to sweet corn this year when the planting season began. The contract he'd just signed guaranteed him a buyer for the corn. He'd been headed to his mom's to see Leigh when he noticed her sedan parked in his driveway. He backed down the rural route rapidly and swung into his long drive.

"Leigh?" He threw his coat on the rack in the foyer but didn't bother to remove his shoes. His eyes scanned the empty living room before he stalked down the dim hallway toward the kitchen. He paused when he saw Leigh standing at the kitchen sink with her hands in soapy water. "What are you doing here?"

Leigh studied him over her shoulder with appreciation. He was wearing a pair of khakis that rode low on his flat stomach and a forest green button down. "You look nice," she said warmly, ignoring his question. He knew full well what she was doing here.

"I had a meeting in Champaign. I was just on my way to Mom's house to see you," he said distractedly as he came up behind her and bracketed her waist in his hands. He leaned down and gave her a kiss that had been hours in building. "But you came to me," he growled out with low masculine satisfaction a moment later as he moved her hair from her neck and planted his lips there.

Leigh leaned her head over to grant his mouth more access to her neck. She sighed with pleasure as he nuzzled her. "Stan was here and he let me in the house. Then I went and spent some time with Ransom in the stable." She turned her head to get Tre's attention as he marauded her neck with his lips. "She's amazing. It was the best gift I've ever received. Thank you again, Tre."

He wanted to tell her that walking into his own house and seeing her casually engaged in such a domestic chore, as if she belonged there, was the best gift he'd ever received. But he didn't want to tell her that and risk her telling him he was a sexist pig, which, knowing Leigh, she just might.

His smile widened at the thought.

"You're more than welcome." He looked out the window over the sink. "Is Stan still out there?" he asked, referring to the full-time farmhand who helped him with his horses.

"No, he left a while ago. Why?" she asked cautiously as she felt him place his hands on her stomach and press her back at the same time he stepped closer to fit his body to her rear end.

He bent his knees and rested his chin on her shoulder. "Because I'm going to make love to you right here, right now, and I wouldn't want anyone to look through the window and see." He spread his fingers possessively over her belly and ground his cock into her ass.

"Tre, I'm doing the dishes," Leigh muttered inanely. In truth, she wasn't even sure what she'd just said. She was hyperfocused on Tre's hands and fingers as they alternated between pressing her into his hard thighs and exploring her shape.

He ignored her. "I love the way you fit me."

Leigh's head fell back into his chest at his statement. Tre was never one to express his feelings much out loud. But what he'd just said, and the low, intense quality of his voice, spoke poignantly to Leigh.

His hand roamed over the curve of her ass before he gripped both of her hips and pulled her back into him. Leigh's damp hands sprang forward onto the counter to catch her upper body. He pressed himself against her, forcing her to feel the extent of his desire.

Leigh moaned longingly. Things felt very full behind the fly of his pants. After last night Leigh's eyes had been opened—wide—at the evidence of just how lusty, potent and energetic Tre could be when it came to sex. Granted, her experience with his type of lovemaking was almost negligible but still, Leigh was a doctor. She knew what was considered to be "normal" when it came to sexual behavior.

But Tre blew away every bell curve about which she'd ever learned.

"When I first saw you leaning over in that stable ten years ago I fantasized about fucking you from behind without so much as a hello," Tre said gruffly near her ear. "Not a very realistic fantasy but a damn hot one. You were sweet-talking poor, helpless King but you were seducing me to a far more profound effect. Do you know how close you were to losing your virginity in those stables that day?"

Leigh moaned softly when he thrust the pillar of his cock in the crevice of her ass. "Very, very close—"

Before she could finish, he leaned over and subjected her mouth to a rapacious kiss. Leigh responded with wild abandonment. She whimpered as he plundered her, establishing his dominance, daring her to deny his right to do so.

"Say it," Tre ordered hoarsely when he dragged his mouth from her entrapping sweetness.

"Say what?" Leigh wondered, befuddled by arousal. Her mouth craned up to try to reach his so that they could continue their intoxicating kiss.

"That you would have let me fuck you that day in the stable," he said with a slow grin. When her lips fell open, Tre had to force himself not to fall on her and drink of the warm honey just behind them. Instead he waited tensely for her to answer.

"I don't think it's a big secret, Tre. We both know I would have if we weren't interrupted."

As if he'd just been waiting for that answer, he reached around and pulled her soft sweater over her head before tossing it on the counter. Her bra landed next to it a second later. He didn't bother removing her skirt, just lifted it up to her waist. Her panties received the same treatment but they went the other direction, down her thighs.

"Spread your legs a little, honey," he instructed. She did so, stopping only when her panties, which were stretched tautly at mid-thigh, prevented her from going further. He smiled as he glanced down at her flagrant beauty, trailing his hand over her thigh high stockings and her bare bottom. He reached into his back pocket to retrieve a condom from his wallet. His eyes flickered up when he saw Leigh twist her head to watch him.

He held her gaze while he unbuckled his belt and shoved his pants and briefs down his thighs.

After he'd rolled on the condom he palmed her pale ass and sent his middle finger into her pussy, testing her. He had to corkscrew his finger into her resisting flesh to be granted entrance but once he stroked inside her an inch or two the dam broke. His eyes glittered with arousal.

"You're so wet down deep," he muttered in gruff appreciation. "Hold still, let me lubricate you."

"Oh...*Tre*," Leigh gasped. He thrust his finger high in her and swept out and up, wetting the delicate folds of her outer sex. She instinctively fell forward further and sent her tailbone higher when he treated her clit to a moist horizontal thrashing. Before she could get used to the overwhelming sensation, he was pressing his cock to her pussy.

He gritted his teeth as he squeezed the head into her juicy, tight channel. Before he thrust, he paused, palming her ass and trailing his hand up the satiny skin at the side of her body. He cradled a firm, suspended breast.

"I'd love to tell you that I'll slow down with you some day, Leigh, but if that day ever comes—which I'm beginning to doubt—it's not going to be anytime soon. Can you take it hard until then?"

Leigh bit her lower lip to stifle a moan. Tre felt like a living furnace behind her. "I'd love to take it hard for as long as you'll give it to me."

He reached up through the thick hair at her nape and fisted a handful. He thrust.

Leigh's head fell back at the gentle pull on her hair. She screamed at the impact of him impaling her, shocked anew at the sensation of being pried apart so ruthlessly only to have him fill the emptiness in the same movement. It felt bestial and primitive in its intensity—it felt sublime.

She trembled as he began to draw in and out of her. As his rhythm quickened and his thrusts became harder, their fevered bodies made a brisk smacking sound that intermingled with their gasping breaths. Just when she tottered on the edge of orgasm, he paused.

"Tre, please," she moaned.

"Hush, honey. You'll like this. Hold your hips steady," he said in a gravelly voice.

He pressed his cock into her to the hilt and reached for her outer sex with both hands. With his left he pinched the lower end of her swollen, tender outer lips together and pressed up slightly, making a warm, wet pocket for her clit. His slid his right forefinger down into the slippery pouch and stimulated the sensitive, hungry piece of flesh with tiny, rapid strokes.

Leigh keened with pleasure. The more he moved the juicier the tiny pocket became until they both could hear the slurping sounds as his finger flicked and rubbed against her clit. Leigh leaned forward until her open mouth was just an inch from the counter and moaned helplessly. The tingling, singeing friction he was building in her was incredible. The soles of her feet began to burn with sexual heat. Her pussy began to vibrate and quiver around his cock even before she came.

"Ahh, God...Tre...please," she gasped, wide-eyed.

Witnessing her honest, uninhibited response was such a turn-on for him. He thrust his hips once, very slowly, not wanting to send her over the edge yet. "Tell me why you would have let me — a total stranger to you — fuck you that day in the stables, Leigh." When she didn't immediately respond, only continued to keen and gasp, he slowed his fingers. Her cries became desperate.

"*Why?*"

"Be-because I'm yours, Tre," she confessed in a quavering voice. Her quaking only amplified when he began to flick her clit again rapidly at the same time that he started to fuck her with short, stabbing thrusts.

She cried out sharply as she came.

When her exquisite spasms around his cock had waned, Tre spread his hands over both of her ass cheeks and squeezed. Not until then did he take her in earnest.

What had he delusionally told himself several days ago — that three good fucks would be sufficient to expunge the poison of Leigh Peyton out of his system once and for all? Right. As he slammed his flesh into her, Tre saw the gross error in his thinking.

Leigh wasn't poison. She was a sweet, addictive elixir that made him hunger for her more and more every time he sated himself on her. Whether her intoxicating essence was healthy or unhealthy for him depended on one thing and one thing alone—whether or not she would choose to give herself to him on a permanent basis.

The vague thought made him go a little berserk when he was already frenzied. He spread the plump cheeks of her bottom so that he could see the tiny, closed bud of her asshole. His forefinger glistened with her abundant juices as he pressed it to her and thrust her back on it, penetrating her in the process. He heard Leigh scream in shocked arousal as she came once again.

His own roar of release followed as he held himself against the furthest reach of Leigh's womb and came thunderously.

For a minute, the silence in the kitchen was broken only by the sound of their gasping, uneven breaths. Eventually, even that gave way to the quiet, but still they remained locked together. He eventually leaned back and watched his finger slide out of her tight, hot hole, and then did the same with his cock from her pussy. He gently raised Leigh and turned her into his arms.

"Hi," she murmured in languid amusement when she looked fully into his handsome face for the first time that day.

He chuckled. "Maybe I didn't get a chance to tell you but I was extremely happy to see you when I walked in that kitchen."

Leigh smiled into his chest. "You told me, Tre."

Chapter Fifteen

☯

Three days later Leigh was helping Sarah clean out her kitchen cabinets when they both heard the side door open and close.

"Take off your boots, Tre!" Sarah called out automatically. She glanced at Leigh and they shared a look of amusement. "Sometimes I wonder who raised that boy."

Tre paused when he entered the kitchen and saw his mother and Leigh sitting on the floor with cans and boxes of dry goods surrounding them. The way they were grinning at him informed him immediately that he was the object of their inside joke.

"What?" he asked cautiously.

"Nothing," Leigh said. She got up from the floor and came over to him. His eyes widened in pleasant surprise when she craned her mouth up and waited for him to lower his head so that they could kiss. They'd spent the last few days exploring each other in many satisfying ways but this was the first time that she'd ever touched him so openly in front of his mother.

"What are you up to?" Leigh asked. She didn't move away when he reached up to stroke her upper arms.

"It's warmer out this afternoon. I thought we might take Ransom out for a ride."

Leigh's eyes sparkled. "That's a great idea. And I bought something to ride in too. Can you just wait until we finish up?"

"Leigh, you go on now. You've been helping me clean all day. You should get out of the house. I'm throwing in the towel myself once I wipe out this cabinet," Sarah insisted.

An hour and a half later she and Tre were riding single-file down the rural route in front of his house. They would both have rather been riding on one of the horse paths on Tre's farm but they were sloppy with melting snow. They had to be cautious of cars on the road. As a result they couldn't ride side-by-side and had to keep at a sedate pace.

Leigh didn't care though. She was too busy appreciating her pretty horse.

"She's amazing, Tre," Leigh called cheerfully over her shoulder. She gave a fake wounded look when she saw where Tre's eyes had been while her back was turned.

"Did you want to ride behind me so that you could stare at my butt?"

A grin tilted one side of his shapely lips. "I didn't want to ride behind you so that I could stare at Ransom's ass."

Leigh laughed uninhibitedly. "You like my Farm & Tackle jeans?"

His smile widened. It did something to him to see her so happy. It had been such a rare sight since he'd known her. He knew that Leigh had understated but very refined taste in clothing. She probably shopped at some of the best boutiques in Chicago. It tickled him to think of her shopping at the Farm & Tackle.

"I'd forgotten how well you fill out a pair of jeans, that's all."

"Thanks," Leigh murmured, sensing his compliment more in his intense blue eyes than in his actual words.

"Leigh?"

"Yeah?"

"When are you planning to go back to Chicago?"

The amusement that had been ghosting her face faded. Her glance fell away from his penetrating stare. Surely he wasn't getting tired of her already, was he? They'd been getting along so well and the sex had been phenomenal.

"I probably should go back tomorrow...the day after at the latest," she said as they turned down his driveway.

"When were you planning on telling me?" He nudged Spartan to move next to Ransom with a subtle movement of his thighs.

Leigh experienced both anxiety and hope when she heard his irritation. So he wasn't tired of her after all? Leigh could only hope that she couldn't be purged too easily from his blood.

"I thought you would get irritated when I told you. And I was right, you are."

Tre exhaled with exasperation. "I'm not mad, Leigh. I know you have a job...a life. I just wish you had brought it up before."

"We'll still be able to see each other. I'll come to visit. You can come to see me in Chicago. I mean...if you want to..."

Tre's mouth pressed into a grim line. He supposed she was right. But for the past ten years he'd dreaded seeing Leigh walk out of his life. He wasn't sure that he'd ever become immune to the experience, even though he knew he'd convinced himself differently hundreds of times.

"You're right," he said shortly after a few seconds. "Let's take care of the horses and go get something to eat. I'm starving."

* * * * *

"Where are we having dinner?" Leigh asked as Tre backed his pickup out of driveway a half an hour later.

"Over at Casey's."

"Ooh. Do we have to? Your mother says they serve garbage over there."

Tre laughed at the disgusted expression on her face. "My mother also thinks that I don't know how to boil water. Haven't you figured out by now that she doesn't believe anybody on the planet can cook better than her?"

"As far as I know, no one can."

"That's beside the point. Casey's serves the best barbecue I've ever had. Everyone in the county knows it too, except for you and my mom." His perceptive eyes slid over to her and examined her averted face. "Oh."

"Oh *what*?"

"Correction. Everyone knows that Casey's has the best barbecue but you, my mom and *your* mother. That's the real reason you don't want to go into Casey's, right, Leigh? Because of the way your mom used to ream out your dad for going there all the time?"

Leigh glanced out the passenger window. "Maybe. She did hate that place," Leigh admitted after a few seconds.

"I'll say," he muttered under his breath.

"What's that supposed to mean?"

"I witnessed her doing it a couple of times. I've never seen anyone demean another human being like that in public. It was a difficult thing for anyone who was at Casey's at the time to watch."

Leigh's face froze.

"She did that?" she whispered slowly. God, if Tre had known about it and he only dropped by Casey's occasionally when he was in town, what had some of the regulars seen?

"I don't want to go there Tre."

His mouth twisted in dissatisfaction as he kept his eyes on the country road. "I've never told you before, Leigh, but I really liked your dad. I know he disappointed you. Hell, I'm disappointed in him to for not being there for you. But because of Doris I think you might not have really known Charlie that well. Just stop in Casey's with me for a quick bite."

When she didn't speak for a moment, he rolled his eyes over to her. "Come on, you'll get to find out how I used to torture myself in moments of self-pity."

That got her attention.

"Okay, but I don't want to stay long," she finally conceded.

Tre was right, Leigh realized as she cautiously entered the country roadside establishment a few minutes later. Casey's wasn't what she expected. Through her mother's bitter diatribes she'd come to picture Casey's as a dark, dingy hole in the wall—the alcohol equivalent of an opium den. Instead Casey's was hopping with business. Patrons included everyone from families to a large table of older women who appeared to be celebrating the birthday of one of their number to young couples on dates. There were quite a few men lining the bar but they hardly appeared to be the emaciated, slurring drunks with whom she'd always imagined her father sitting shoulder to shoulder.

"Hey, Tre," a chubby blonde woman in a waitress's apron greeted him as she set a menu in front of Leigh.

"Hey, Sheila."

"Don't have to give him one, he always gets the same thing," Sheila explained to Leigh good-naturedly as she tilted a thumb at Tre. She started. "Why, you're Charlie Peyton's little girl, aren't you?"

Tre confirmed the waitress's statement with a brief introduction. Leigh jumped in surprise when Sheila Kaufman shouted loudly toward the bar.

"Hey Joe, Alex, guys. Look who's here. It's Charlie Peyton's girl!"

Leigh gave Tre a repressive look when the large bartender and several men at the bar turned to study her.

"Well I'll be," the bartender muttered. Leigh tried to gather herself when it became clear that four men plus the bartender were coming over to their booth.

The bartender reached her first and offered a warm grin and a beefy handshake. "Pleased to meet you, little lady. I'm Joe Casey, the owner of this fine establishment. Down for a visit from the Windy City are you? I hear it gets pretty cold down there by where you live so close to the lake. But it's close to that hospital you work at…what's it called?"

"Memorial," Leigh answered dazedly. Then she remembered her manners. "It's nice to meet you, Joe. How- how did you know where I live?" she wondered. The next man answered her when he stepped up enthusiastically to shake her hand.

"Alex Gardner, Leigh. We all know about you because you were Charlie's favorite topic of conversation. Real proud of you, he was."

"And with good reason. Harry Micklin, Leigh." Harry glanced over at Tre with raised eyebrows. "How's a slacker like you come to be squiring around such a pretty lady, Tre?" Harry teased before the next man elbowed him aside so that he could meet Leigh.

Leigh politely spoke to every man but her shock was evident on her face when they casually revealed intimate details of her life, like how she'd fallen off a slide in the third grade and broken her arm to how she had graduated with her undergraduate degree magna cum laude.

After a moment Joe Casey finally took in her overwhelmed expression and herded the men back toward the bar. "Let these young people eat their dinner in peace, guys," he barked. "Sheila, what are you bringing them?"

"Oh, I'll just have what Tre's having," Leigh told Sheila distractedly when the waitress looked at her. Sheila nodded warmly and winked at Tre once before she waddled off.

"We hope you'll come back and see us sometime soon, Leigh. We all miss Charlie like crazy. He was a good friend," Joe said.

"Thank you. I will come back sometime. I-I'm glad that my father had such nice friends, Joe," Leigh said awkwardly. But Joe's warm smile told her that he didn't mind her disorientation.

Tre saw that her eyes were moist when they were alone again. "I'm sorry, honey. I just thought you might want to know..."

"I do. Don't apologize, you were right, Tre," Leigh said with a shaky laugh. "That was really weird."

He smirked. "Wait until you see the side of the cash register."

"What?"

He didn't have the opportunity to answer her question before Sheila briskly set down two bottles of beer in front of them. Leigh pick up hers bemusedly, examined it then took a drink. Her brow wrinkled and she took a bigger gulp. "I can't believe my father bragged about me. I never knew he cared that much."

"He should have been telling you how proud he was instead of these people down here," Tre murmured softly before he tilted his bottle of beer to his mouth. "To be honest with you I got the impression that Doris had him convinced he wasn't worthy of you. But he always worshipped you from afar, Leigh." His smile stretched wide when he recognized the truth of his own words. No wonder he'd always shared such an affinity with Charlie.

"Here you go, you two," Sheila said as she plopped down two plates of food unceremoniously. "Enjoy!"

Leigh scowled when she lifted the bun off her sandwich. "There's coleslaw on my barbecue."

"Just eat it," Tre said around a bite. "It's good."

She looked doubtful but she was so hungry she took a bite anyway. Her eyes widened in surprised appreciation.

"Told you so."

Leigh didn't even bother to respond to his smugness. Her mouth was too full with a huge second bite.

"Do you want to say goodbye?" Tre asked twenty minutes later as they stood up from the booth.

Leigh nodded and followed him to the bar.

"How'd you like your barbecue, Leigh?" Joe Casey called out when he saw her.

"It was fantastic. I'll definitely be back for more."

"Hey, maybe next time you come you can bring a more recent picture to put up," Alex Gardner piped up enthusiastically.

"Excuse me?" Leigh murmured. Her eyes flew to Tre's like he was an interpreter and Alex was speaking a foreign language. Tre just nodded across the bar. She stared. Pictures of Leigh at every age were affixed to Casey's cash register with magnets. Leigh saw her third, fifth and eighth grade school photos along with her high school and University of Illinois graduation pictures. There was a picture of her and Deana Waters when they were inducted into the National Honors Society when they were juniors in high school. Leigh's brow crinkled in wonderment when she saw one of her proudly holding up what she knew to be her acceptance letter to Northwestern Medical School.

Although Joe Casey was a large, plainspoken man, that didn't mean that he wasn't sensitive, Leigh realized. He cleared his throat when he noticed Leigh's expression. "Charlie brought them in over the years, Leigh," he said quietly. "Truth be told we've all became a tad bit taken with you." He raised his bushy eyebrows and gave Tre a pointed stare.

"We never had any pictures of Charlie. So after he died we kept them up out of respect for him. But I guess it must be a little bit of a shock for you to walk in and see that. Reckon I can hand them all over to you tonight. They're yours, after all."

Leigh was so preoccupied that she didn't notice Alex's sound of protest or Tre's answering scowl that silenced him immediately.

"Do you want them, Leigh?" Tre asked after a moment.

Leigh blinked out of her trancelike state and met Joe Casey's eyes. "No. I mean, unless you want me to take them. But I'll make sure I bring in a picture of Charlie next time, Joe."

"What are you thinking about, Leigh?" Tre asked when they got into the truck. Her answer took him by surprise.

"I didn't realize I looked like such a dork when I was growing up."

He gave a sharp bark of laughter. "Hey, I happen to like those glasses. They matched your braces almost perfectly. All that shiny metal in such a pretty face, those little boys must have been dazzled back then."

She snorted. "I did look like I was about ready to sink my nose into a book a second after the flash went off in every picture," she muttered.

"Yeah, your brainy looks are the real reason guys like Alex Gardner would have thrown a fit if Joe took down those pictures." He grinned when he saw her small smile.

"Tre?"

"Yeah?" he asked as he started the truck and pulled out of the parking lot.

She swallowed convulsively. "Those pictures aren't what you were referring to, were they? About how you would torture yourself in rare moments?"

Tre didn't speak for several long seconds.

"They might have been," he said impassively after a long pause.

She stared out the side window, feeling both glad and bereft at his admission. Happy because he'd just admitted that he'd suffered seeing reminders of her and knowing that she wasn't in his life. Empty because she heard that coldness in his voice—that distance that she knew without logical proof still stood as a significant barrier between them. Why was he filled with so much ambivalence about her?

When Tre parked the car in his driveway Leigh glanced out at the stables. "I'm glad I got to ride Ransom before I go."

He frowned into the darkness then clicked open the truck door. "Let's go inside, Leigh. I need a shower. Care to take one with me?"

Her eyes widened. She nodded eagerly.

Chapter Sixteen

Tre didn't pull her into the shower until he'd gotten it good and steamy. They shared the soap, lathering up each other's bodies with a sensual playfulness that didn't take long to turn into hot, greedy lust.

Leigh had just finished soaping up his back and was starting on his muscular ass. She lathered him up and then squeezed the taut flesh with relish. She grinned impishly as she tried to bounce his tense butt up and down like he was wont to do with her bottom. He looked down at her over his shoulder, his eyes sparkling with mirth.

"Not working, is it?"

Leigh snorted with laughter as she palmed his hard curves again greedily. "There's got to be fat on your butt to make it bounce. Your ass is as hard as a rock." She massaged the round, hard muscles appreciatively. No wonder he could fuck her with such explosive strength with these muscles powering his hips. When he started to turn around she stopped him with a hand at his waist.

"Where do you think you're going? I'm not done playing," she warned him seductively as she glided her fingers between his buttocks. "Squeeze," she whispered against his damp back.

He complied before he laughed. "Kind of an X-rated playground, don't you think?"

Leigh pressed her mouth to his warm, smooth skin.

"Hmmm, you're right, I think it is. Let go of my hand, Tre, I can't move it," she said wryly. She waited until he'd released her fingers from the tight clamp of his glutes before she swept her fingers down the furrow and between his thighs. Her fingertips caressed his round, full testicles.

Inspired, she brought back her hand, ignoring his sound of protest, and created a rich lather with both hands at once. Her left hand snuck back between his hard thighs to massage his balls while the other went around his hips to spread the foam along the shaft of his tumescent cock. Just the sight and feeling of him made warm liquid bubble from her sex. She stroked him from balls to tip several times slowly, using her sensitive fingertips to skim across the path of several swollen dark blue veins. Meanwhile she squeezed a taut testicle gently and watched Tre's face for a reaction.

When he growled in tense, primitive arousal, she knew she'd found the pressure he preferred.

"Jack me harder," he demanded. He watched as her tight fist and supple wrist began to pound down over his cock in the rhythm that he'd taught her so many years ago. Tre experienced an elemental urge to spill himself in her hand, just like he had back then in the lake. One hand rose to cradle Leigh's neck tenderly. He felt her gaze on his face after he'd endured another minute of her merciless pumping.

"Don't stop. I plan on coming," he said starkly.

He clenched his eyes shut after a moment and did just that.

Leigh stared at the powerful image of him coming almost silently, only small, muffled grunts exuding from his throat at the same tempo that his body quaked with pleasure. His nipples pulled into tight, tiny bullets. His first shot of cum spurted powerfully forth several inches but Leigh caught the rest with her pumping fist. After she'd milked every last drop that he had to give her, she kissed his side softly.

Tre's eyes flickered open. He smiled down at her. "That felt good," he rasped.

Leigh pressed her flushed cheek into his flesh. "I thought maybe it did," she said as she smiled into his wet, warm skin.

Come To Me Freely

"Are you ready to have the favor returned?"

She glanced up. Her clit pinched with arousal at the satisfied but far from sated expression in his penetrating blue eyes.

She nodded eagerly.

He reached up and tilted the showerhead down so that it didn't spray them directly. He sat on the bench at the back of the luxurious shower, pulling her after him. "Turn around and bend over."

"Spread your thighs more," he ordered as he put his hands on her damp, warm ass, spread his legs and inched her back closer to his mouth. He felt her go still when he pressed her ass cheeks up and back.

"Bend all the way over, honey. Grab your ankles," he told her thickly as he massaged her flesh.

When she'd positioned herself the way he wanted, he leaned forward and sniffed her pussy appreciatively. His nostrils flared. He tilted his face, gripped her ass tightly, pinning her into place, and plunged his tongue deeply into her pussy. Her juices flowed around him, wetting his nose and chin. He held her steady and sank deep, vibrating his tongue as high as he could go in her warm channel before he began to draw in and out with relish.

He closed his eyes and fucked her with his tongue for a suspended period of time, losing himself in her heat and taste. When he heard her low, desperate moans he opened his eyes and slid his tongue out of her. He studied her with heavy eyelids. It was no wonder she was moaning in misery. Her clit hung down between her lips, red, swollen and needy.

"Do you want to come?" Tre said thickly.

"Yes," she whispered desperately against her thigh.

He reached for the damp bar of soap and circled it in his right hand. He pinned back her ass cheeks with the other, exposing her tightly clasped, tiny asshole to his gaze. She gasped in surprise when he pushed his soapy thumb into her. He felt her start in surprise.

"Hold still," he soothed as he steadied her and began to draw in and out of her tight opening. God, she was on fire in there. He stiffened his thumb and slid the entire length in and out of her.

"Does it feel good?" He saw her open her lips but the only thing that came out was a low, uneven moan.

He took that for a yes.

In order to bolster his assumption he pressed his face into her and lashed her suspended clit with his long tongue. He heard her cry out as the first wave of orgasm crashed into her. He continued to alternate his movements between a rapid, flicking motion and a hard, relentless press. His thumb plunged into her harder.

He needed to get inside that hot little hole.

Leigh continued to moan plaintively even after the convulsions of her powerful climax had slowed. She felt like every nerve ending along her sacrum—everything from the top of her clit to her pussy to her ass—tingled with awakened energy, hungry for more friction. If Tre hadn't stood up at that moment and pushed her until her hands went down to where he'd just been sitting, Leigh probably would have begged him single-mindedly to fuck her.

She'd been made that uninhibited by sheer horniness.

Leigh heard him tilting the showerhead again and felt some of the warm water spraying her calves and lower thighs. She turned her chin on her shoulder, watching Tre when he came to stand behind her. Her eyes widened hungrily.

He lathered up his cock in his hand. His entire arm moved back and forth over his length. He'd acquired more than a respectable erection once again. The image made her mouth sag open with lust. His eyes glittered up at her when he heard her small, wanting cry.

"I'm going to fuck your ass, honey."

Leigh licked her lower lip anxiously as her hot gaze continued to pin his enormous erection. It had made her hornier than hell when he'd finger-fucked her asshole while they were in the midst of passion for the past few days. She'd be lying if she said she hadn't thought about what it would be like to take his cock there. But now that the opportunity was before her—or behind her, in this case—uncertainty mingled with her anticipation.

He lathered up his right hand generously with soap before he set down the bar. As he moved between her legs he saw the anxiety in her forest green eyes. "You're not sure about this?"

Leigh bit her lower lip.

"Would you just let me play with you a little and then tell me what you decide?" he asked. He waited tensely. He would do whatever she wanted of course but he hoped he could convince her. Maybe it was because of the fact that Leigh had said she would be leaving any day now. Tre couldn't be sure. All he knew was that an emotional intensity was growing in him, a thick, potent brew. And he wanted...no, *needed* to take Leigh in this primitive, intimate way.

Leigh just nodded her head, speechless. Before she'd tilted down her chin twice, Tre spread his hand over her bottom and sent his forefinger into her ass. He groaned at the same time she did. There was no doubt about it. He had to get into that smooth, tight channel. She radiated heat around his finger as he plunged it in and out of her. When he heard her aroused cry he squeezed his second to her little hole.

"Push back, Leigh. It will go in easier that way," he whispered hoarsely. He watched as she backed into him and the closed rosette of her ass opened to accept him. Once he was inside he glided in and out of her easily. He gazed up at her, trying to gauge her reaction. When he heard her low moan he held her bottom steady with one hand and began to fuck her with his fingers.

Leigh tilted her head back and closed her eyes. How was it that his stimulation in her ass could awaken so many different erogenous zones in her body? Her nipples pebbled into tight, achy points. The nerves in the soles of her feet gave off a burning sensation that somehow required a release. Her juices wet her thighs. And the heat and friction building in her clit felt unbearably good.

"Tre...my...please touch me," she said as her hips began to move in a counter rhythm to his fucking fingers.

He bent slightly over her, appreciating the feeling of his erection brushing against the silky skin of her ass. "Take another finger and I'll make you come."

"Yes."

He gave a small smile at the evidence of her arousal. Leigh had an ass that had given him the cruelest, most merciless hard-ons since the day he'd first laid eyes on her. If she allowed him to fuck it once in a while he'd die a happy man.

If she allowed him to more than once in a while, he'd live a truly blessed life.

She groaned low in her throat when she backed onto Tre's thumb in addition to his first two fingers. Tre held his hand steady when she paused, gasping, but when the small stab of pain had faded, Leigh thrust her bottom back until she'd taken their full lengths. Her head fell forward at the impact of feeling so full. Tre was true to his word though. While she panted heavily he worked his left hand between her thighs. He went straight for the kill, rubbing his forefinger along the valley of her sex lips, stimulating her clit hard.

When he heard Leigh's peaking cry he pinched and vibrated the tender flesh until she screamed full-throatedly. Maybe it was a little unfair but he spoke to her while she was still in the full throes of orgasm.

"I'm going to put my cock in you now, honey." Hearing her cry out in orgasm, feeling the abundance of her warm juices against his finger and experiencing the shimmering vibrations of her climax in her ass was enough to drive him to the brink of insane lust.

Leigh heard him distantly as pleasure swamped her. The quality and sheer power of the new sensations that were surging through her felt overwhelming. She suddenly understood how it would be possible for a woman to choose to become a slave for sex. Her body pulsed and zinged with not only pleasure but pure, vibrant life.

The feeling was intoxicating.

So she was no longer afraid when she felt him press his cock to her ass. It felt far too wide but when he gruffly ordered her to push back on him she did. She was so hungry…ravenous for him…for Tre.

She gasped when the tip of him slid into her ass. Pain splintered through her but it faded almost immediately.

Tre paused, recognizing that her harsh exhalation hadn't come from pleasure. He stood very still with his throbbing shaft in his hand while the head was being squeezed in agonizing pleasure by the tight ring of Leigh's rectum.

Leigh panted heavily, mouth open, staring blindly at the tile wall in front of her. After a moment she realized the pain was gone, only to have been replaced by a low-level burn that was echoed in her clit.

"More," she whispered.

Tre was only too happy to comply. They both pushed and several inches of his lathered cock breached her. They both groaned in unison. She felt so good gloving him that he began to fuck her gently with the portion that had been fortunate enough to be surrounded by her heat thus far.

"Ahh, God, Tre!" Leigh shouted out. She didn't feel like he was just fucking her. It felt like something more, something unknown. All she knew was that she had an overwhelming desire to be possessed by him completely. She pressed back gently but firmly when his pumping motions became more rapid. He grunted with tense appreciation when he sank further into her.

After a few more instances of pause and withdraw, only to bury his eager flesh further into her on reentry, Tre's balls nested warmly in her lush ass cheeks. He growled deep in his throat at the small—but immensely rewarding—victory.

Leigh continued to gasp harshly through an open mouth when she felt Tre pause after he was fully sheathed in her body. Surely it wasn't possible to harbor such a large pillar of flesh inside of her ass and for it to feel so good...for her to want nothing but the friction of a good fuck. She whimpered softly when Tre leaned forward carefully and kissed her shoulder.

"Are you okay?" he rasped.

"Yes."

They both made a sound of desperation when his cock leapt eagerly in her tightly clasping channel.

"I'm going to fuck you a little in here. Then I want to take you to my bed to finish."

Leigh's eyes blinked open dazedly. His heart hammered even more rapidly beneath her breast. He hadn't ever said anything overtly to her and she'd instinctively known that he didn't want to speak of it. They'd made love in practically every room of his house and even lustily in the stables on several occasions.

But this was the first time he'd ever suggested making love in his bed.

All thoughts of whether or not she should be happy or concerned about this latest development were expunged from her mind when he began to fuck her, slowly at first, experimentally.

"That's right, just relax," he soothed.

It was a hypocritical thing to say of course, because he was tenser than a coiled spring as he slid in and out of her. Sweat stung his eyes but he forced himself not to blink. The image of his cock plunging in and out of her ass was spellbinding.

When he realized that his thrusts were growing more demanding though, and that Leigh was moaning in a deep, throaty, sexy manner, he gritted his teeth and drew out of her slowly. His eyes glittered as the head of his cock slid out of her and the hole that he'd so carefully opened began to slowly seal shut.

But her magical entry would open again for him, and this time with much more ease. He helped her to stand and drew her under the water. While the spray rinsed them he leaned down over her and kissed her ravenously. His fingers trailed over her hip and irrevocably back to her ass.

He sent a finger up inside of her and fucked her at the same cadence that he plunged his tongue into her mouth. When Leigh pressed the tips of her pointy breasts into his lower chest and scraped her nipples against him he moaned gutturally and pulled her tightly to him. By slow degrees he came to the realization that he'd been pleasurably sidetracked. He palmed an ass cheek roughly and then smacked the firm, plump flesh. Did Leigh really think her ass was fat? As far as he was concerned her ass was fucking perfect. Speaking of which...

"Let's go to the bedroom to finish."

Leigh nodded. When she paused in his bedroom a moment later, after they'd dried off, Tre told her to get on her hands and knees on the bed. He watched her between desire-laden eyelids as he fumbled in his bedside table for a bottle of lubricant.

She'd positioned herself to take him into her body—into her life—once before on this very bed.

The thought made his mouth form into a grim line.

He came up behind her on the bed, leaning over her to pull forward several pillows. He layered them beneath her shoulders.

"Press your tits to the pillows, Leigh, and put your arms out in front of you," he directed. The sight of her plump ass sticking up in the air made his cock leap up eagerly. "Are you comfortable?"

"Yes," Leigh assured him as she turned her cheek into the pillow. In fact, she'd never felt so vulnerable in her life and that certainly pitched her sexual excitement up several degrees. It crested with alarming speed when Tre reached between her legs and sent two thick fingers forcefully into her drenched pussy and began to fuck her with no preamble.

Tre never took his eyes off her as she keened in surprised pleasure, pouring a generous amount of lubricant directly onto his cock before he dispersed it over his heavy, achy erection with his hand. He spread her fleshy bottom.

And with much less ceremony than he had the first time around, he began to sink his cock into her ass.

Leigh made a strangled sound in her throat at the dual stimulation in her ass and in her pussy. She pressed back on him desperately, feeling his wide cock penetrating her...possessing her.

She turned her flushed face into the pillow and came.

When she came back to herself a moment later it was to find herself being steadily fucked by Tre. He was showing her relatively little gentleness or mercy now. Not that she wanted to be treated with kid gloves, because this felt so damn good. She began to bounce her bottom back on him, loving the feeling of his teeming cock in her flesh, relishing in the sounds of his throaty grunts and growls of intense arousal.

When his thighs began to slap against her ass she gripped the bedding and held on for dear life. A blur of dichotomous messages set her body and brain alight. She couldn't say the overwhelming sensation was pleasant as he fucked her as hard as he often did her pussy, but the feeling was something she desired...something that felt imperative to her.

She loved being the recipient of his wild, stormy energy, even if she wouldn't have been able to sustain it for long.

A loud shout seemingly ripped out of his throat. She clearly felt his cock throb and pulsate deep inside her body. Her eyes widened with disbelief. It was the most erotic thing she'd ever experienced. She'd never felt nearer to his raw, elemental masculinity.

She reached back and slid her fingers against her needy clit. Soon her own sharp cries of pleasure were mingling with his harsh groans.

Tre blinked the sweat out of his eyes several moments later. Something had just happened. His passion for Leigh had just burned and scored not only his body but his spirit and his defenses, leaving nothing untouched, least of all his stormy emotions.

Fury began to rise in him, unexpected and potent. He abruptly withdrew from Leigh and turned her onto her back. He waited until her startled gaze met his eyes.

"How could you have done it, Leigh? How could you have married Jim, knowing full well what was between us?"

Her breath drew in raggedly. Had she just missed something? From where had this sudden bitterness...no, *fury* stemmed? Her heart seemed to shrivel in her chest when she slowly recognized that it had been there all along in him. *That* was the reserve that she always sensed in him...the coldness...the anger that always seemed to brew in the distance like a thunderstorm on the horizon. He'd never unleashed its full force.

Until now.

"I loved Jim," she said shakily. "Not like I love you but like a brother and a good friend. And he needed me."

"Because he had a spinal cord injury? So what...you would have been with me instead of him if I was a paraplegic?" Tre asked, eyes blazing incredulously.

"No. I mean he *needed* me. You never did," Leigh defended.

"The *fuck* I didn't!" Tre shouted so abruptly that Leigh started.

He swung his legs around and moved to the edge of the bed. For a panicked second Leigh thought that he was going to leave the room. Her jaw stiffened with a shadow of the pain and anger that Tre was feeling.

"You sure picked a funny way of showing me how much you needed me. Leaving without a word, never contacting me, barely ever visiting, moving to another state… Yeah, it's a real wonder that I assumed you didn't want me, let alone need me!"

Leigh cringed when he whipped his head around and she saw the pure wildness in his expression. "*You're* the one who made an art out of avoiding me. *You're* the one who begged me not to tell your precious Jim about us." He leaned toward her ominously. "And *you're* the one, princess, who decided to take the easy path and never show on that afternoon before I went back to San Diego."

Leigh's brow crinkled. "I didn't mean that we should never tell Jim. I just didn't want us to do it fresh from getting out of bed with each other," she said slowly. "And I don't know what you're talking about, showing up here on the day you returned to the Navy. I never saw you before you left. You just vanished out of my life."

Tre just stared at her for several long seconds.

"So according to your personal version of reality," he began darkly, "I made it clear how crazy I was about you, told you that I was willing to risk losing my relationship with my brother so that I could be with you and then just blithely jumped on a plane the next day and forgot about you? Is that right, Leigh? Do I have it all straight?"

"Pretty much, yeah. And stop yelling at me!" She didn't seem to notice that her own voice volume was escalated nearly as much as his was. "And that's not my *personal* version of reality. That's what happened. All except that part about me thinking you forgot me. I didn't think that. I always knew you...wanted me in bed. That was one of the few things you made clear to me."

"Well I would have made it a lot clearer if you had shown up here that day. But you didn't, did you? Instead you avoided me for the first of many times to come over the next ten years." Tre's volume had lowered but the contempt in his voice more than made up for it.

"Maybe you're the one who is living in your own reality. You never asked me to meet you here on the day you went back to the Navy."

"You knew. I looked all over town for you and couldn't find you that morning. First I looked for you here on the farm but L.J. said that you'd called in sick for detassleing that day. Then I went to your house and Doris told me that you weren't home. I went back to Mom and Dad's. You weren't there but I told Jim that I was looking for you. I made an excuse about riding Kingmaker one last time. He said that you two were going to register for classes at the University of Illinois later in the morning but that he'd pass on the message. I even left a written note with him. Jim said that he was picking you up to leave for Urbana in an hour or so and that he would give it to you then. I waited here at the farmhouse until six. I almost missed my plane out of O'Hare that night because at the time I was so certain that you were going to show up..."

For the first time since he'd started to speak, he took in how pale Leigh had become and felt the first stirrings of misgiving.

"What's wrong?" he finally asked slowly.

"They never told me," she said. "Jim and I didn't register for classes that day you left. I'll remember that day you left for as long as I live. We didn't register for school until the week afterward." Her eyes glazed in memory.

"I was there at the house when you came," she said slowly. "I had to have been. My mother lied to you. I didn't go in for work because I felt so upset that you were leaving and about how much it was going to hurt Jim when we told him the truth. As the day wore on it started to dawn on me that you weren't going to contact me before you left. Every day that went by without hearing from you surprised me a little, until the days became weeks and the weeks, years."

Tre could hear his heart begin to thrum loudly in his ears. "I asked Jim afterward...I specifically asked him if he gave you the note that day."

Leigh glanced up at him. Her face had a waxy, unnatural quality to it that spoke of shock. "What did he say?" she asked slowly.

He gave a dazed shrug. "He said yes, Leigh. He told me that he'd told you and given you the note but that you had said that you didn't think there would be time after you registered and checked out the campus. He never did?"

His only answer was a weary smile.

He watched her get up from the bed in rising disorientation. "What are you doing?" He felt completely off-balance at that moment. But his awareness sharpened when he saw Leigh head toward the bathroom.

"My clothes are in here."

The fact that her voice sounded almost matter-of-fact alarmed Tre more than anything. It didn't match with the pale, shell-shocked quality of her face. He lunged after her but she shut the bathroom door before he could restrain it with his hand.

"Leigh, open this door," Tre growled in frustration.

Her voice sounded calm enough from within the bathroom. He heard her turn on the water faucet. "Just a second, Tre." When she opened the door two minutes later she was dressed in her jeans and sweater. She wouldn't make eye contact with him.

"I need to go. Can you take me to Sarah's?"

"What?" Tre asked incredulously. "Leigh...what the hell? This is a shock to both of us. But isn't it a good thing that we found out? That now we know that neither of us ever really betrayed the other?"

Her impassive response chilled him.

"I always knew, deep in my heart, that I was unfaithful to him. Never mind that it wasn't with my body. I was unfaithful with my heart and soul. I used to worry that somehow Jim knew about how I felt about you. I didn't think it was possible but still...it always nagged at me that maybe that was the real reason behind his depression.

"And it was true," she whispered. "He *did* know. Somehow he knew that we'd fallen in love. That was why he lied to us. All along he knew. What a funny way for me to confirm my suspicions about it all," she murmured as she stared out the window with a strange, bemused expression on her face.

She blinked heavily.

"Can you take me back now, Tre?"

Her gaze looked lifeless. Dread trickled through him as he began to realize he was going to lose her...again. "No. You're in shock, honey." He tried to reach for her but she backed away elusively then moved past him toward the front door.

"Fine. It's not that far. I'll walk."

Tre grasped her upper arm firmly and forced her to face him. His emotions were chaotic. But the one that he recognized most at that moment was fear. "All right, damn it, I'll drive you to Mom's. But tomorrow we need to talk about—"

Leigh shook her head. "No. Not tomorrow."

His helplessness transformed into fury.

"God damn it, Leigh, *when* then?" he bellowed.

"I don't know," she replied honestly before she turned and walked out of the bedroom.

Chapter Seventeen

When Tre heard the shrill shout behind him he almost just kept walking to his pickup without turning. The two bags of groceries he was carrying were heavy—maybe because they mostly contained beer. He felt like cracking one of the cans open before he slowly faced the irritated-looking woman who raced to overtake him in the Food King parking lot.

Alcohol had been the only way that Charlie Peyton could cope with having to deal with Doris Peyton day in and day out. Tre suddenly felt acute sympathy for the man.

Of course, he was finding that his own alcohol consumption had increased more than he preferred in the past two months as well. But in his case it was because he was forced to deal with the glaring absence of Doris Peyton's daughter.

All in all, Tre believed that Charlie'd had it better than he did. At least Leigh would have likely returned his phone calls.

He didn't speak or alter his cold expression when Doris finally came within range of him.

"You couldn't leave well enough alone, could you? I remember all those years ago, the way you tried to take Leigh away from Jim. I can't say that it surprised me that a selfish son of a bitch like you wouldn't give two thoughts about betraying his own brother or seducing a young, innocent girl—"

"If you want to say something relevant to me, say it now. I'm not standing here while you rant."

Doris' pale cheeks flushed with anger.

"How is it even *possible* that you and Jim were brothers? *He* listened to me when I told him that he'd be doing Leigh the biggest favor of her life by keeping her away from you...even if she was foolish enough to think she cared about you. I told Jim that your idea of caring about a woman lasted for about as long as it took for you to have your fill of her in bed. And I was right too! Just look at what you've done to my daughter. I just saw her and she's a mess...all because of your self-serving—"

Tre temporarily forgot his anger at the fact that Doris and Jim had actually knowingly conspired together when he heard the last sentence. He stepped forward aggressively.

"What the hell do you mean you just saw Leigh?"

Doris flinched slightly. Before she could form a likely excuse, however, she was looking at Tre McNeal's back.

"Hold on, you hothead. Don't you have any decency? Just because my daughter is fool enough to get herself mixed up with the likes of you doesn't mean you have to encourage her corruption. Aren't there enough women in this town willing to spread their legs for you? She's your sister-in-law for Christ's sake, and now look what you've done to her!"

Tre turned around, jaw hard and eyes blazing. "The only thing I've done to her is fall in love with her, you witch. Where is she?"

Doris's chin came up stubbornly.

"Fine. Have it your way, Doris. You kept us apart once but it's not going to happen again." He turned to leave but his head swung around when he saw her knowing expression.

"You're not going to look so smug when Leigh and I have our first child and you're about as welcome at our home as you are at every other house in this town."

He walked away then, knowing he'd probably regret the cruel statement later but thoroughly satisfied in the moment at the blank look of shock on Doris' face that his off-the-cuff insult had inspired. But as he got in his truck and peeled out of the parking lot he couldn't help but wonder if he wasn't the one who was being smug by assuming that Leigh had returned because she'd decided she wanted them to be together...finally.

* * * * *

Leigh almost left the stables when she heard a car door slam heavily in the driveway. But a sense of calm acceptance had come over her ever since she'd spoken to her mother earlier...even before that. Tre likely was ready to strangle her for avoiding him for the past two months but she'd needed the time to sort through things. She stroked Ransom's velvety nose and praised her in a low, soothing voice.

She heard the noise of boots crunching in the gravel a minute later and immediately recognized the sound of Tre's long-legged, confident tread, his impatience made clear by the scattering gravel. Her heartbeat began to thrum loudly in her ears.

Okay, maybe she wasn't as calm as she'd thought.

He called out her name the second he had the stable door partially opened.

"I'm here, Tre...with Ransom." Even though she got the impression that he'd been impatient to find her a second ago, he paused in the open doorway, the bright spring sunlight behind him casting him in shadow.

"Why are you so skinny? Aren't you eating?"

Her laugh was husky and low, making what felt like a low grade electrical shock run over his skin. He came into the stable slowly when he heard that mesmerizing sound, closing the door behind him, casting the stable once again into dimness.

"I've been eating, Tre," she assured him softly, knowing him well enough by now that his brusque question actually came from concern. She watched him as he drew nearer to her, her hand still on Ransom's nose. He looked thinner as well, and his angular jaw hadn't seen the edge of a razor for at least twenty-four hours. Nevertheless, she thought she'd never seen anything half as beautiful as he looked to her at that moment.

"Guess you drove down to see Ransom," he said laconically.

Tre watched through narrowed eyelids as she turned to face him. Had he said she was thin? He supposed that she was. Her waist and face did look thin, especially when compared to just before she'd left the farm, after she'd put on a few much-needed pounds from his mother's good cooking. But her breasts looked delectably full beneath the simple white button-down shirt that she wore with a pair of faded jeans.

"You'd guess wrong then, Tre." Ransom whickered softly behind her and nudged Leigh's shoulder. A flicker of a smile twitched his sculpted lips.

"You haven't been feeding that horse sugar, have you?" he asked with mock sternness. He was close enough now to see that her eyes glittered in the dim light as she looked up at him. His arms itched to hold her.

As if she'd read his mind she murmured his name brokenly and flew straight into them.

Tre dropped his head so that his face pressed to the side of her soft hair. He inhaled her scent. His eyes burned when he closed them. "Why'd you come, honey?" he asked finally.

"Because I wanted to be with you," Leigh murmured into his hard chest. "Because I couldn't stand being apart from you for another night."

He didn't speak for several moments. The hand that rose to cradle the back of her head shook slightly. Relief struck him powerfully, akin to the sweeping, abrupt pleasure of orgasm. She hadn't come here to tell him to stop bothering her and leave her alone. Only after a minute did Tre recognize the emotion that lingered—it was joy, pure and powerful. He leaned back so that he could better see her face.

"You wouldn't return my calls. I knew guilt must be eating you up inside. What happened, honey?"

She shrugged, unsure of how to put her transforming feelings into words. "I still feel a little guilty. I probably always will. But—I hate to say it, Tre—Jim was wrong for what he did too. I know that he loved me and that he needed me. But he shouldn't have lied to get what he wanted. I spoke to my mother earlier today. I went to confront her about lying to you that day ten years ago when she claimed I wasn't in the house. Do you know what she told me? She said that she and Jim talked about it—about keeping us apart."

"I know," Tre said. "I just saw Doris in town. That was how I knew you were here."

Leigh's chin tilted down thoughtfully. "You know what an honest, genuine person Jim was."

"I thought I did."

"I think that maybe that was what got to him the most, in the end. Knowing how he'd deceived us," Leigh whispered.

Tre's hand finally rose and caressed the side of her neck. "I think maybe you're right. It doesn't surprise me for a second what Doris did. But Jim's actions were totally out of character for him. I've even wondered if he wasn't being manipulative when he asked me to go with him to get that drug. I'd like to think that he wasn't. But if he did mean it as a message for me to back away from you it had to be one of the cruelest things he'd ever done. It felt like torture to sit in that doctor's office, knowing what he was planning."

"Tre," Leigh murmured. Her delicate facial features were tight with his shared pain. She'd never seen Tre look so vulnerable. Her arms encircled his waist as she tried to confer comfort. She felt safer speaking into his chest.

"That was something I never told you about Jim and I. He wanted us to have sex in that way. But I just couldn't do it. When we were in college and we became so involved in the spinal cord injury groups I learned that there's a certain...ethic, or politically correct way, that the associations educate people about sex. They encourage both the person with the spinal cord injury and their partners to re-evaluate and rebuild the way they think of sex. It's the same way that I would educate people about their injuries and sex today."

"I know. Maybe Jim never told you but I sat in with him for a couple sessions with a psychologist when he was in rehab. They talked about the problems that arise if the person with spinal cord injury keeps obsessing about sex being equated with the penis and with penetration."

"Oh," Leigh blinked in surprise. Jim had never told her about Tre's involvement in that aspect of his rehabilitation. "I guess I don't need to explain too much about that then. What I wanted to tell you was that I became much more invested in that particular philosophy than Jim did. He wanted to use the drug to have sex. I refused. It seemed sort of...obscene to me. The person with the spinal cord injury doesn't have any sensation, can't move. I saw it as being in direct opposition to the shared, mutual gratification inherent to lovemaking."

Tre saw how much she struggled emotionally. It slowly dawned on him that what she was saying somehow directly related to her guilt about Jim.

Leigh glanced up at him, seeming to gain strength from his presence. "But the thing of it is, Tre...after being with you in February, after falling even deeper in love with you than I did ten years ago and then discovering for certain that Jim knew about us I started to wonder if..." Her head fell forward on his chest. "I started to wonder if I resisted him so much for my own selfish reasons. Maybe I unconsciously thought of having sex in that way with Jim as the ultimate betrayal..."

"To us? To me?" Tre asked starkly. She nodded, her averted face into his chest.

"Honey, you're one of the smartest people I know. Even if you did feel about Jim the same way you feel about me I think you would have told him the same thing. I don't think you held so firmly to those principles you teach people just to meet your own ends for a second."

Leigh tilted her head back and met his gaze. "You don't have to reassure me, Tre. I already came to that same conclusion. It just took me time. I'm sorry if I caused you to suffer in the meantime." She saw him raise one dark brow.

"As long as this is the decision that you came to then the suffering was worth it,"

Leigh saw that his small grin reached all the way to his blue eyes. She realized with awe that she was currently feeling his love for the first time without the barriers of his anger and hurt. She hugged him tightly, surrounding herself in it. It only took her half a minute to feel his customary heat radiating through their clothes.

"Let's go inside. I want to make love to you," he said.

"I want to, Tre, but I'm kind of grimy. It was a long drive. I should shower."

"You know I don't give a damn about that. I love the way you smell." He turned his head and inhaled the distilled fragrance at her neck deeply. It paradoxically both soothed his spirit and made his cock stiffen unbearably with excitement.

Leigh chuckled as she caught his gaze, which was quickly segueing from warm to hot. "Maybe so but you have a really warped sense of smell. Remember how sweaty I was in Grandpa's house ten years ago? And you said you liked the way I smelled then."

"I didn't like it. I loved it," Tre corrected gruffly. "Don't get me wrong, I usually don't go in for sweaty women." His smiled widened when Leigh snorted in amusement. "But your sweat on the other hand must have some kind of special hormones in it that definitely bypass the brain and go straight to my cock."

"Tre."

"It's true. I was just as sweaty as you were that day," Tre murmured quietly. "You didn't seem to mind it either."

Her lips fell open. He was right, of course. To her, Tre had smelled and tasted like the very essence of desire. She blinked once, then twice to break the spell he was weaving over her so effortlessly.

"Are you planning on bending me over a stall and fucking me in the stable, Tre?" she murmured, knowing by now how much he liked to do that after spending that week with him in February.

His eyes flashed with prurient interest. "Now *that* sounds like a good idea," he grinned when he saw her exasperated look. "But I suppose I can hold out for long enough for you to shower now that I know you're not going to be making any permanent exits from my life," he added with a narrow look.

"I won't be going anywhere for awhile now, Tre. And when I do, I'll let you know when you'll be seeing me again. Is that good enough?"

"I suppose it'll have to be," he murmured contentedly before he sank his head and covered her mouth with his.

Also by Beth Kery

&

eBooks:
Come To Me Freely
Exorcising Sean's Ghost
Fire Angel
Fleet Blade
Flirting in Traffic
Groom's Gift
Subtle Lovers: Subtle Voyage
Subtle Lovers 1: Subtle Magic
Subtle Lovers 2: Subtle Touch
Subtle Lovers 3: Subtle Release
Subtle Lovers 4: Subtle Destiny
Through Her Eyes

Print Books:
Exorcising Sean's Ghost
Fleet Blade
Naughty Nuptials *(anthology)*
Subtle Lovers 1: Subtle Magic
Subtle Lovers 2: Subtle Touch
Subtle Lovers 3: Subtle Release
Subtle Lovers 4: Subtle Destiny

About the Author

ஐ

Beth Kery grew up in a huge house built in the nineteenth century, where she cultivated her love of mystery and the paranormal. When she wasn't hunting for secret passageways and ghosts with her friends, she was gobbling up fantasy novels and any other books she could get her hands on. As an adult she learned about the vast mysteries of romance and sex and started to investigate that phenomenon thoroughly, as well. Her writing today reflects her passion for all of the above.

ஐ

The author welcomes comments from readers. You can find her website and email address on her author bio page at www.ellorascave.com.

Tell Us What You Think

We appreciate hearing reader opinions about our books. You can email us at Comments@EllorasCave.com.

Why an electronic book?

We live in the Information Age—an exciting time in the history of human civilization, in which technology rules supreme and continues to progress in leaps and bounds every minute of every day. For a multitude of reasons, more and more avid literary fans are opting to purchase e-books instead of paper books. The question from those not yet initiated into the world of electronic reading is simply: *Why?*

1. *Price.* An electronic title at Ellora's Cave Publishing runs anywhere from 40% to 75% less than the cover price of the exact same title in paperback format. Why? Basic mathematics and cost. It is less expensive to publish an e-book (no paper and printing, no warehousing and shipping) than it is to publish a paperback, so the savings are passed along to the consumer.

2. *Space.* Running out of room in your house for your books? That is one worry you will never have with electronic books. For a low one-time cost, you can purchase a handheld device specifically designed for e-reading. Many e-readers have large, convenient screens for viewing. Better yet, hundreds of titles can be stored within your new library—on a single microchip. There are a variety of e-readers from different manufacturers. You can also read e-books on your PC or laptop computer. (Please note that Ellora's Cave does not endorse any specific brands.

You can check our website at www.ellorascave.com for information we make available to new consumers.)

3. ***Mobility.*** Because your new e-library consists of only a microchip within a small, easily transportable e-reader, your entire cache of books can be taken with you wherever you go.

4. ***Personal Viewing Preferences.*** Are the words you are currently reading too small? Too large? Too... ANNOYING? Paperback books cannot be modified according to personal preferences, but e-books can.

5. ***Instant Gratification.*** Is it the middle of the night and all the bookstores near you are closed? Are you tired of waiting days, sometimes weeks, for bookstores to ship the novels you bought? Ellora's Cave Publishing sells instantaneous downloads twenty-four hours a day, seven days a week, every day of the year. Our webstore is never closed. Our e-book delivery system is 100% automated, meaning your order is filled as soon as you pay for it.

Those are a few of the top reasons why electronic books are replacing paperbacks for many avid readers.

As always, Ellora's Cave welcomes your questions and comments. We invite you to email us at Comments@ellorascave.com or write to us directly at Ellora's Cave Publishing Inc., 1056 Home Avenue, Akron, OH 44310-3502.

Discover for yourself why readers can't get enough of the multiple award-winning publisher

Ellora's Cave.

Whether you prefer e-books or paperbacks, be sure to visit EC on the web at www.ellorascave.com

for an erotic reading experience that will leave you breathless.

CPSIA information can be obtained at www.ICGtesting.com
Printed in the USA
LVOW12s2324041114

411992LV00001B/48/P